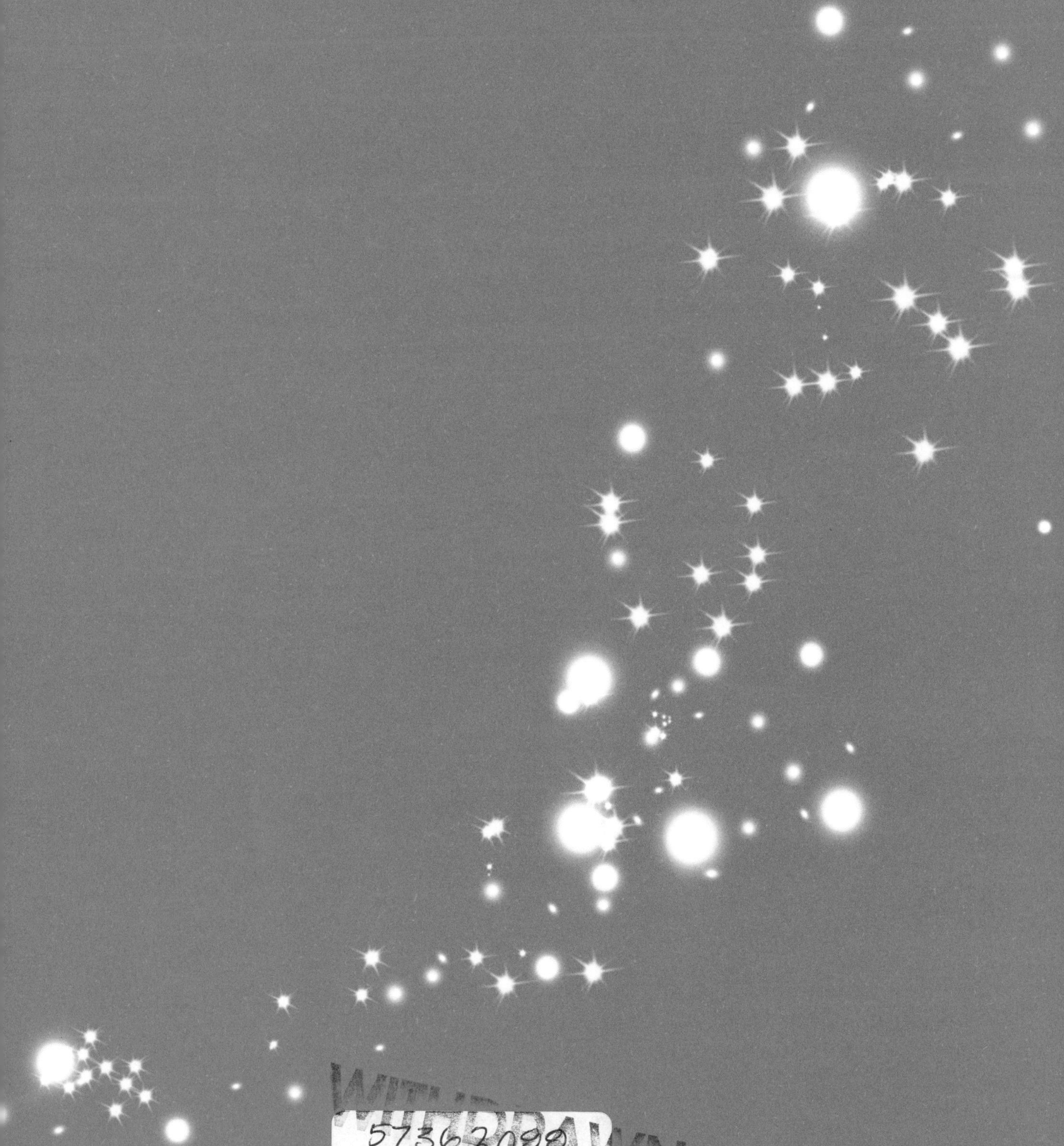

SYBIL
the Backpack Fairy

2

"AMANITE"

MICHEL RODRIGUE • Writer
ANTONELLO DALENA & MANUELA RAZZI • Artists
CECILIA GIUMENTO • Colorist

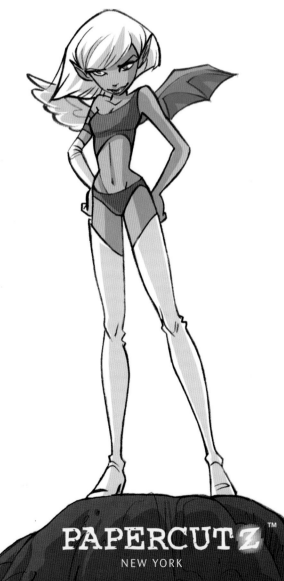

PAPERCUTZ™
NEW YORK

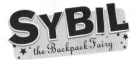

SYBIL the Backpack Fairy GRAPHIC NOVELS AVAILABLE FROM PAPERCUTZ

SYBIL
the Backpack Fairy
1
"NINA"
Rodrigue
Dalena
Razzi
PAPERCUTZ

1 "NINA"

SYBIL
the Backpack Fairy
2
"AMANITE"
Rodrigue
Dalena
Razzi
PAPERCUTZ

2 "AMANITE"

COMING SOON!

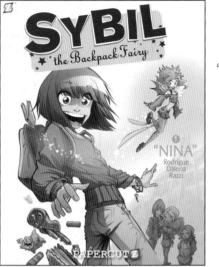

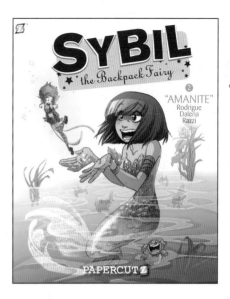

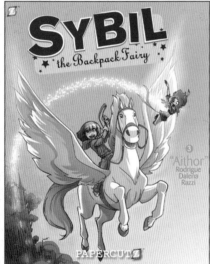

SYBIL
the Backpack Fairy
3
"Aithor"
Rodrigue
Dalena
Razzi
PAPERCUTZ

3 "AITHOR"

SYBIL THE BACKPACK FAIRY
graphic novels are available in hardcover
for $11.99 each, from booksellers everywhere.

Or order from us: please add $4.00 for postage and handling for first book ordered, and add $1.00 for each additional book. Please make check payable to NBM Publishing. Send to: Papercutz, 40 Exchange Place, Suite 1308, New York, NY 10005 or call 800 866 1223 (9-6 EST M-F) MC, Visa, AmEx accepted. www.papercutz.com

Sybil the Backpack Fairy
#2 "Amanite"
Michel Rodrigue – Writer
Antonello Dalena & Manuela Razzi – Artists
Cecilia Giumento – Colorist
Joe Johnson – Translation
Tom Orzechowski – Lettering
Production by Nelson Design Group, LLC
Associate Editor – Michael Petranek
Jim Salicrup
Editor-in-Chief

ISBN: 978-1-59707-305-9

Printed in China
March 2012 by New Era Printing LTD
Trend Centre, 29031 Cheung Lee St.
Rm. 1101-1103, 11/F, Chaiwan, Hong Kong

Distributed by Macmillan
First Papercutz Printing

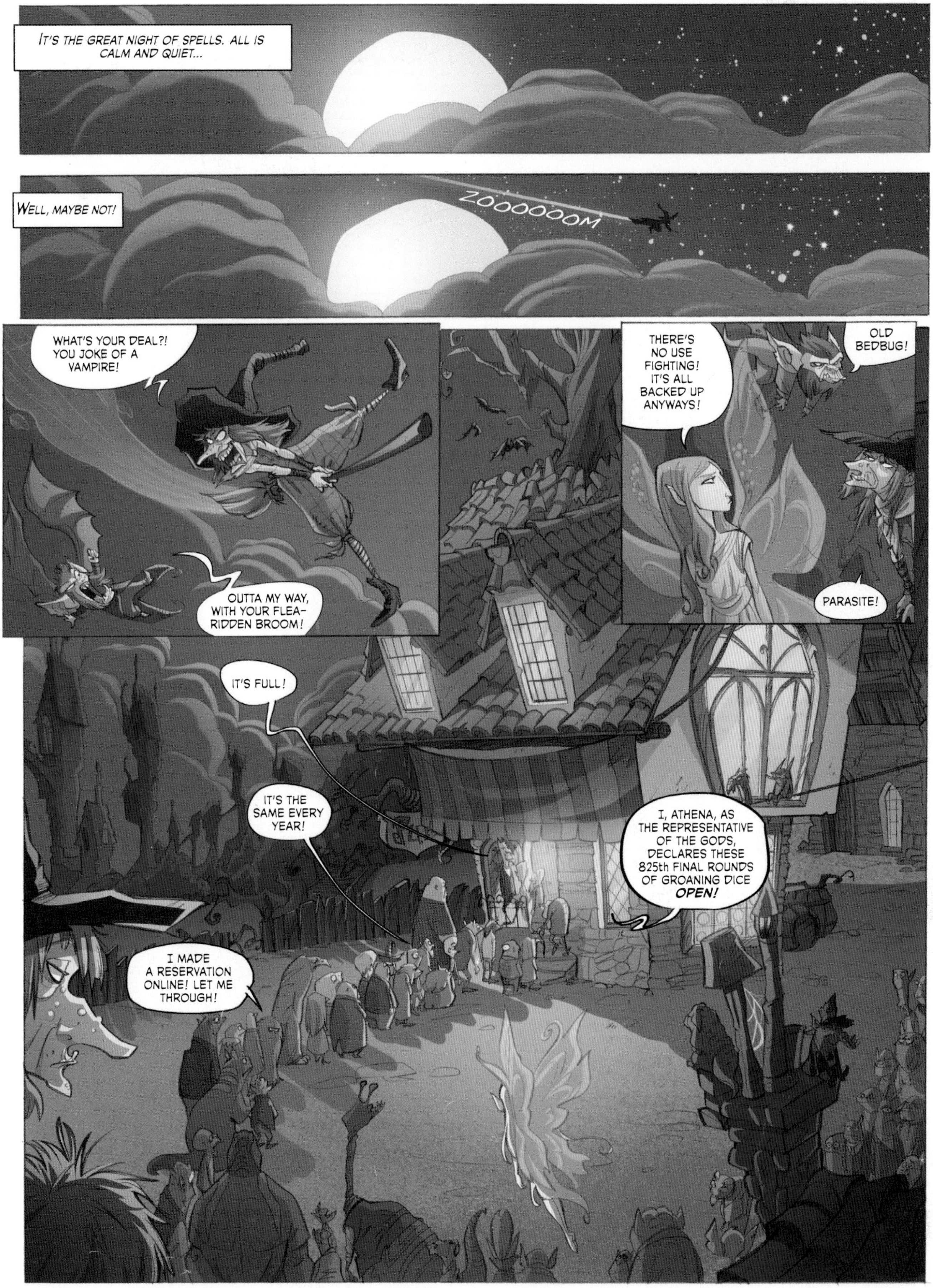

IT'S THE GREAT NIGHT OF SPELLS. ALL IS CALM AND QUIET...
WELL, MAYBE NOT!
ZOOOOOOM
WHAT'S YOUR DEAL?! YOU JOKE OF A VAMPIRE!
OUTTA MY WAY, WITH YOUR FLEA-RIDDEN BROOM!
THERE'S NO USE FIGHTING! IT'S ALL BACKED UP ANYWAYS!
OLD BEDBUG!
PARASITE!
IT'S FULL!
IT'S THE SAME EVERY YEAR!
I, ATHENA, AS THE REPRESENTATIVE OF THE GODS, DECLARES THESE 825th FINAL ROUNDS OF GROANING DICE OPEN!
I MADE A RESERVATION ONLINE! LET ME THROUGH!

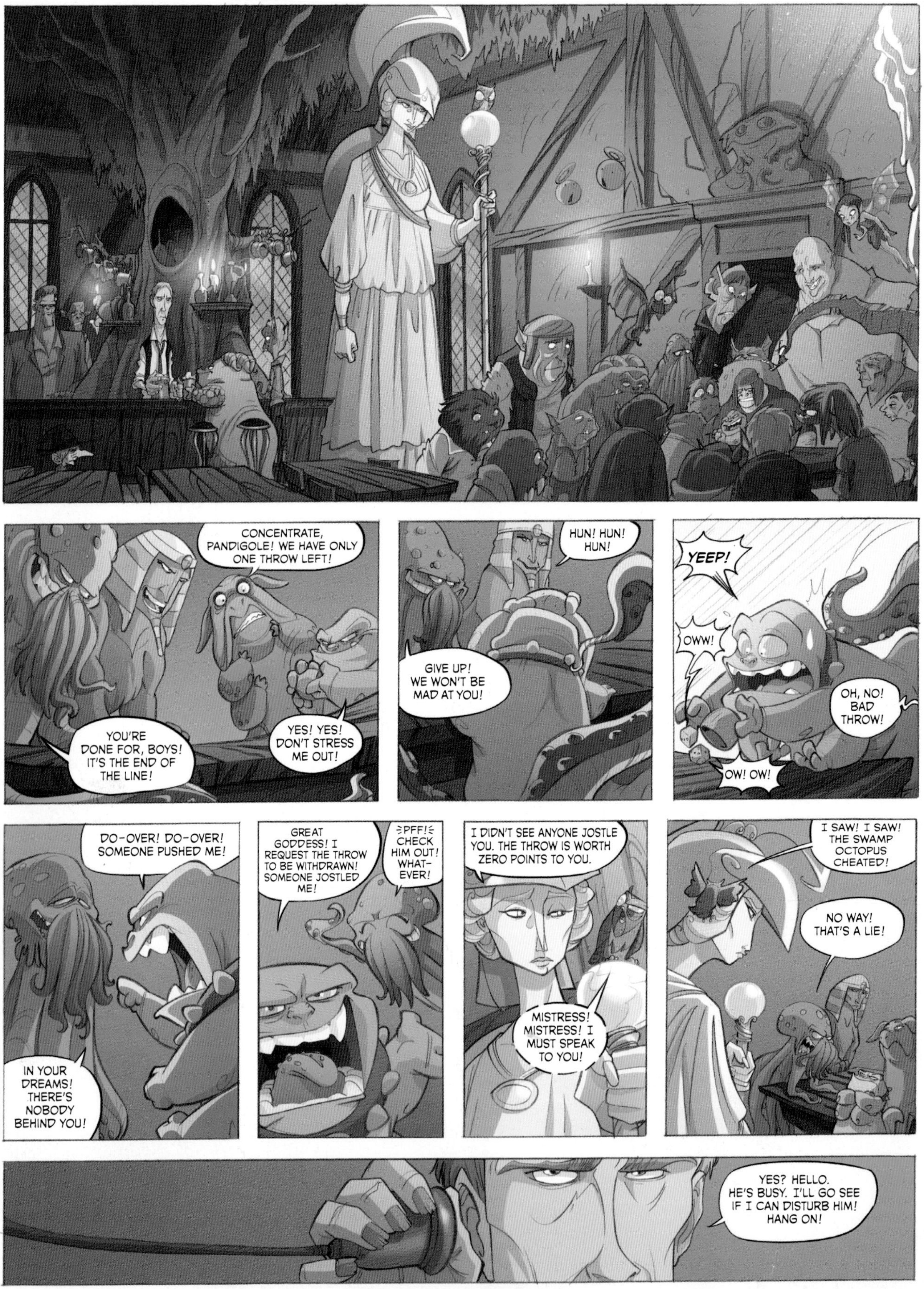

CONCENTRATE, PANDIGOLE! WE HAVE ONLY ONE THROW LEFT!
YOU'RE DONE FOR, BOYS! IT'S THE END OF THE LINE!
YES! YES! DON'T STRESS ME OUT!
HUN! HUN! HUN!
GIVE UP! WE WON'T BE MAD AT YOU!
YEEP!
OWW!
OH, NO! BAD THROW!
OW! OW!
DO-OVER! DO-OVER! SOMEONE PUSHED ME!
IN YOUR DREAMS! THERE'S NOBODY BEHIND YOU!
GREAT GODDESS! I REQUEST THE THROW TO BE WITHDRAWN! SOMEONE JOSTLED ME!
PFF! CHECK HIM OUT! WHAT-EVER!
I DIDN'T SEE ANYONE JOSTLE YOU. THE THROW IS WORTH ZERO POINTS TO YOU.
MISTRESS! MISTRESS! I MUST SPEAK TO YOU!
I SAW! I SAW! THE SWAMP OCTOPUS CHEATED!
NO WAY! THAT'S A LIE!
YES? HELLO. HE'S BUSY. I'LL GO SEE IF I CAN DISTURB HIM! HANG ON!

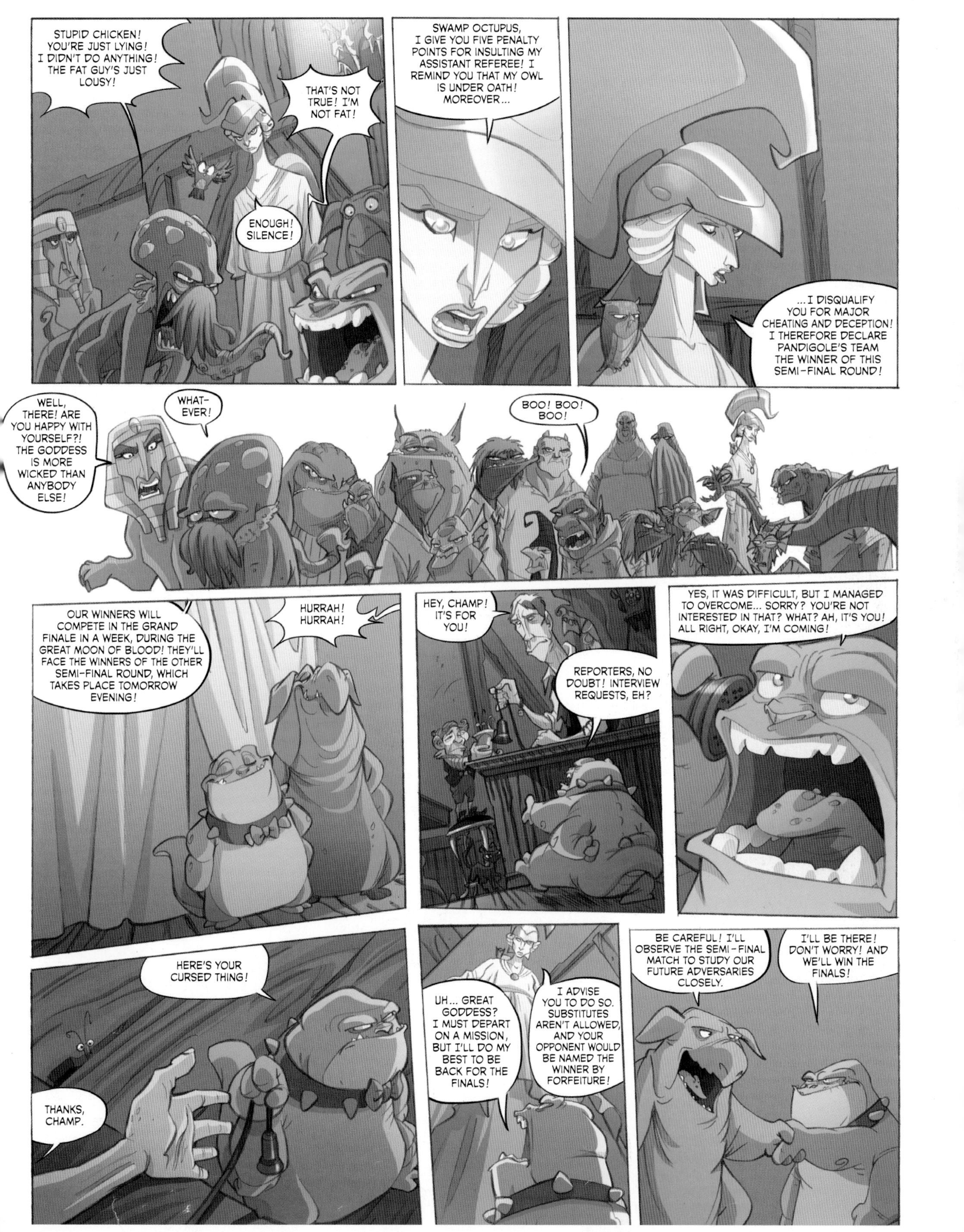
STUPID CHICKEN! YOU'RE JUST LYING! I DIDN'T DO ANYTHING! THE FAT GUY'S JUST LOUSY!
THAT'S NOT TRUE! I'M NOT FAT!
ENOUGH! SILENCE!
SWAMP OCTUPUS, I GIVE YOU FIVE PENALTY POINTS FOR INSULTING MY ASSISTANT REFEREE! I REMIND YOU THAT MY OWL IS UNDER OATH! MOREOVER...
...I DISQUALIFY YOU FOR MAJOR CHEATING AND DECEPTION! I THEREFORE DECLARE PANDIGOLE'S TEAM THE WINNER OF THIS SEMI-FINAL ROUND!
WELL, THERE! ARE YOU HAPPY WITH YOURSELF?! THE GODDESS IS MORE WICKED THAN ANYBODY ELSE!
WHAT-EVER!
BOO! BOO! BOO!
OUR WINNERS WILL COMPETE IN THE GRAND FINALE IN A WEEK, DURING THE GREAT MOON OF BLOOD! THEY'LL FACE THE WINNERS OF THE OTHER SEMI-FINAL ROUND, WHICH TAKES PLACE TOMORROW EVENING!
HURRAH! HURRAH!
HEY, CHAMP! IT'S FOR YOU!
REPORTERS, NO DOUBT! INTERVIEW REQUESTS, EH?
YES, IT WAS DIFFICULT, BUT I MANAGED TO OVERCOME... SORRY? YOU'RE NOT INTERESTED IN THAT? WHAT? AH, IT'S YOU! ALL RIGHT, OKAY, I'M COMING!
HERE'S YOUR CURSED THING!
THANKS, CHAMP.
UH... GREAT GODDESS? I MUST DEPART ON A MISSION, BUT I'LL DO MY BEST TO BE BACK FOR THE FINALS!
I ADVISE YOU TO DO SO. SUBSTITUTES AREN'T ALLOWED, AND YOUR OPPONENT WOULD BE NAMED THE WINNER BY FORFEITURE!
BE CAREFUL! I'LL OBSERVE THE SEMI-FINAL MATCH TO STUDY OUR FUTURE ADVERSARIES CLOSELY.
I'LL BE THERE! DON'T WORRY! AND WE'LL WIN THE FINALS!

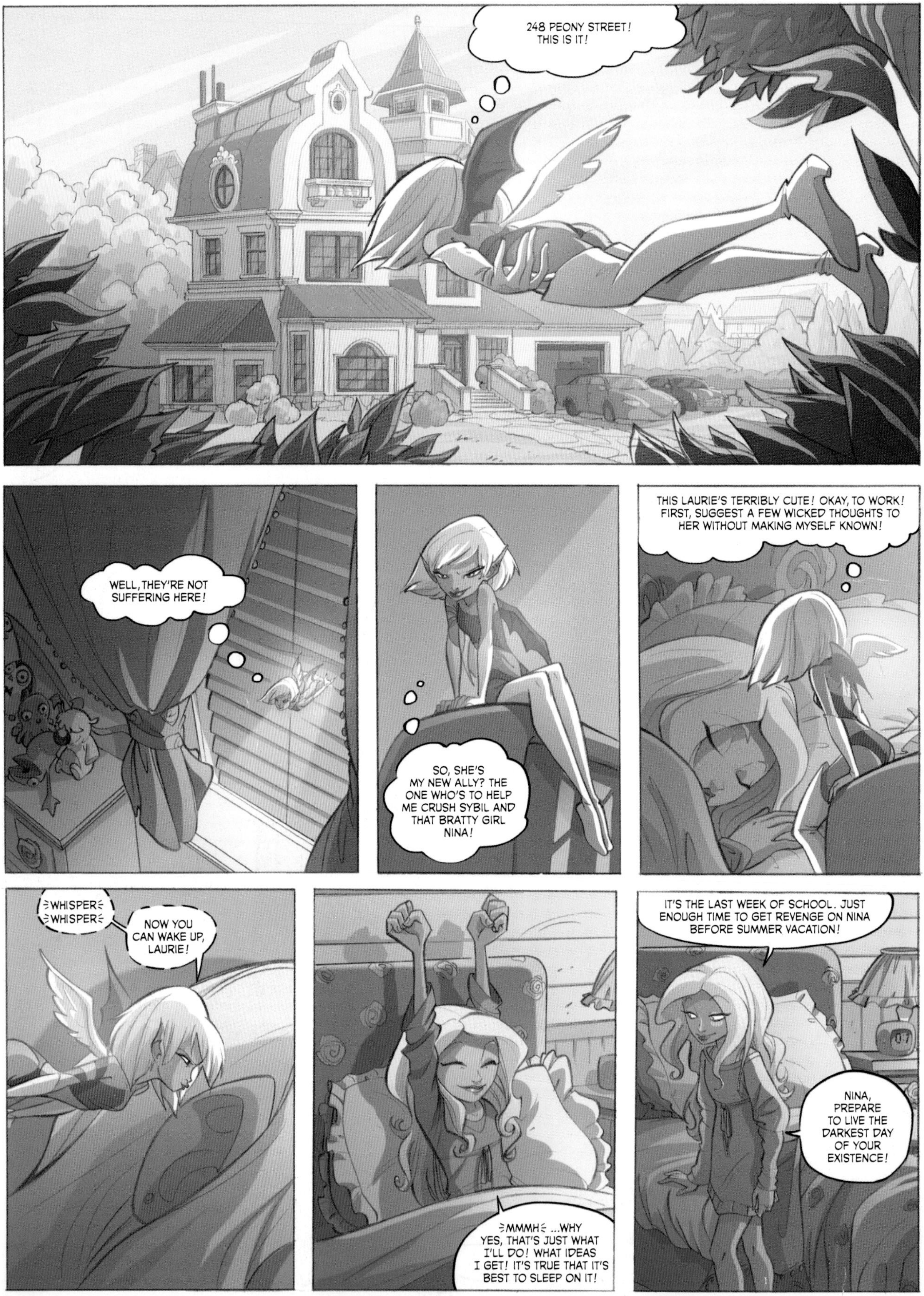

248 PEONY STREET! THIS IS IT!
WELL, THEY'RE NOT SUFFERING HERE!
SO, SHE'S MY NEW ALLY? THE ONE WHO'S TO HELP ME CRUSH SYBIL AND THAT BRATTY GIRL NINA!
THIS LAURIE'S TERRIBLY CUTE! OKAY, TO WORK! FIRST, SUGGEST A FEW WICKED THOUGHTS TO HER WITHOUT MAKING MYSELF KNOWN!
WHISPER WHISPER
NOW YOU CAN WAKE UP, LAURIE!
MMMH ...WHY YES, THAT'S JUST WHAT I'LL DO! WHAT IDEAS I GET! IT'S TRUE THAT IT'S BEST TO SLEEP ON IT!
IT'S THE LAST WEEK OF SCHOOL. JUST ENOUGH TIME TO GET REVENGE ON NINA BEFORE SUMMER VACATION!
NINA, PREPARE TO LIVE THE DARKEST DAY OF YOUR EXISTENCE!

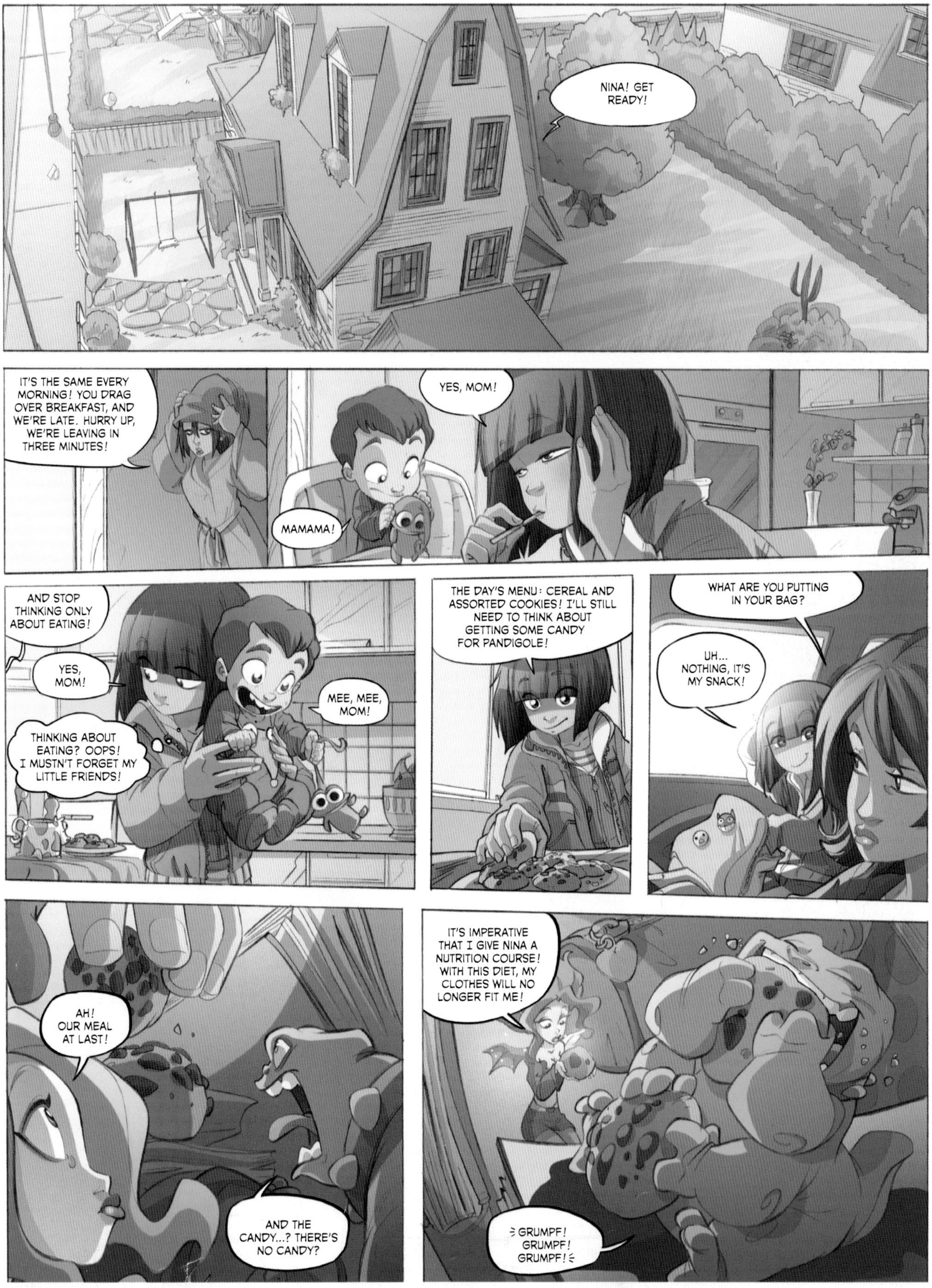
NINA! GET READY!
IT'S THE SAME EVERY MORNING! YOU DRAG OVER BREAKFAST, AND WE'RE LATE. HURRY UP, WE'RE LEAVING IN THREE MINUTES!
YES, MOM!
MAMAMA!
AND STOP THINKING ONLY ABOUT EATING!
YES, MOM!
MEE, MEE, MOM!
THINKING ABOUT EATING? OOPS! I MUSTN'T FORGET MY LITTLE FRIENDS!
THE DAY'S MENU: CEREAL AND ASSORTED COOKIES! I'LL STILL NEED TO THINK ABOUT GETTING SOME CANDY FOR PANDIGOLE!
WHAT ARE YOU PUTTING IN YOUR BAG?
UH... NOTHING, IT'S MY SNACK!
AH! OUR MEAL AT LAST!
AND THE CANDY...? THERE'S NO CANDY?
IT'S IMPERATIVE THAT I GIVE NINA A NUTRITION COURSE! WITH THIS DIET, MY CLOTHES WILL NO LONGER FIT ME!
GRUMPF! GRUMPF! GRUMPF!

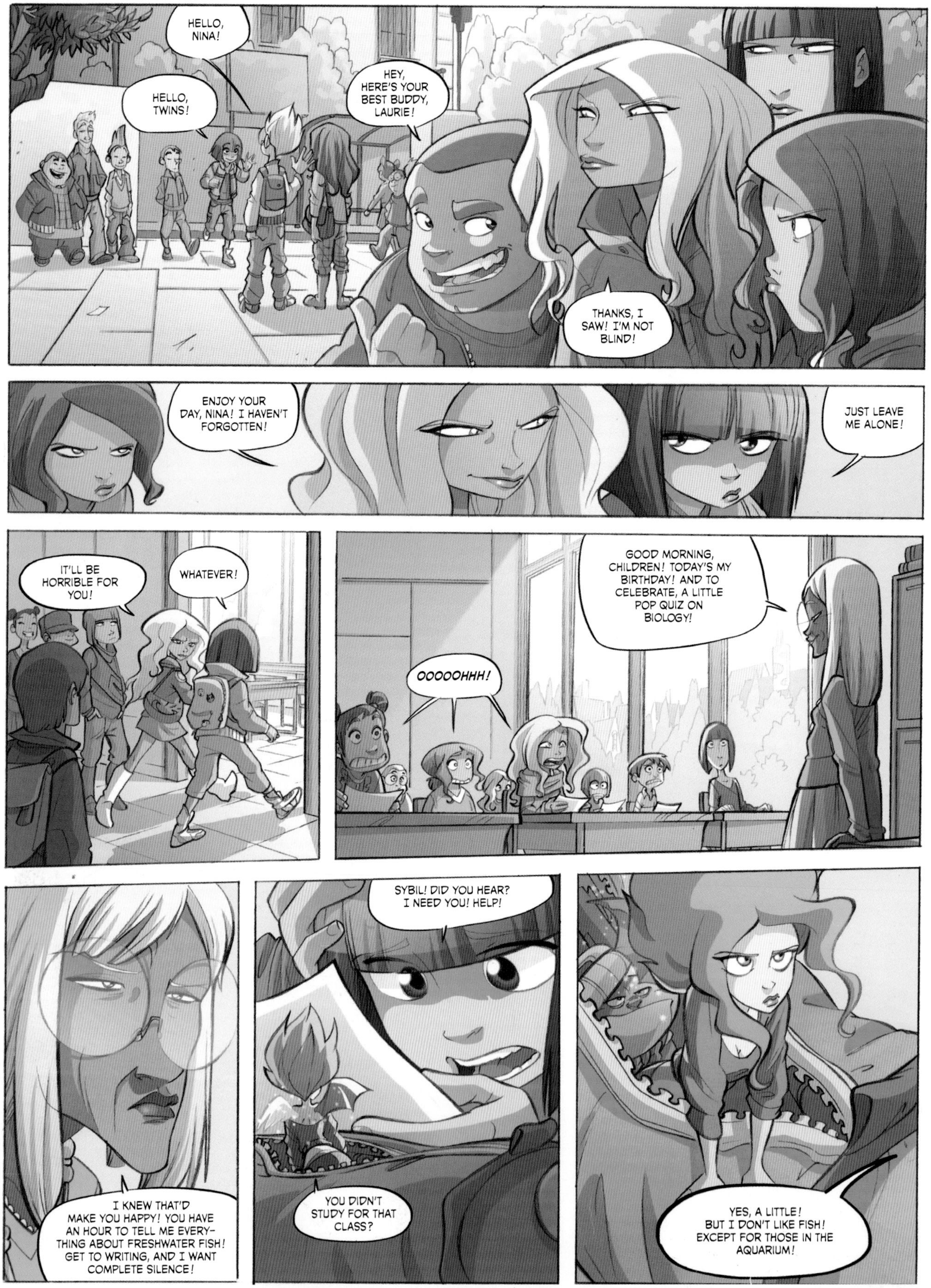
HELLO, NINA!
HELLO, TWINS!
HEY, HERE'S YOUR BEST BUDDY, LAURIE!
THANKS, I SAW! I'M NOT BLIND!
ENJOY YOUR DAY, NINA! I HAVEN'T FORGOTTEN!
JUST LEAVE ME ALONE!
IT'LL BE HORRIBLE FOR YOU!
WHATEVER!
GOOD MORNING, CHILDREN! TODAY'S MY BIRTHDAY! AND TO CELEBRATE, A LITTLE POP QUIZ ON BIOLOGY!
OOOOOHHH!
I KNEW THAT'D MAKE YOU HAPPY! YOU HAVE AN HOUR TO TELL ME EVERY-THING ABOUT FRESHWATER FISH! GET TO WRITING, AND I WANT COMPLETE SILENCE!
SYBIL! DID YOU HEAR? I NEED YOU! HELP!
YOU DIDN'T STUDY FOR THAT CLASS?
YES, A LITTLE! BUT I DON'T LIKE FISH! EXCEPT FOR THOSE IN THE AQUARIUM!

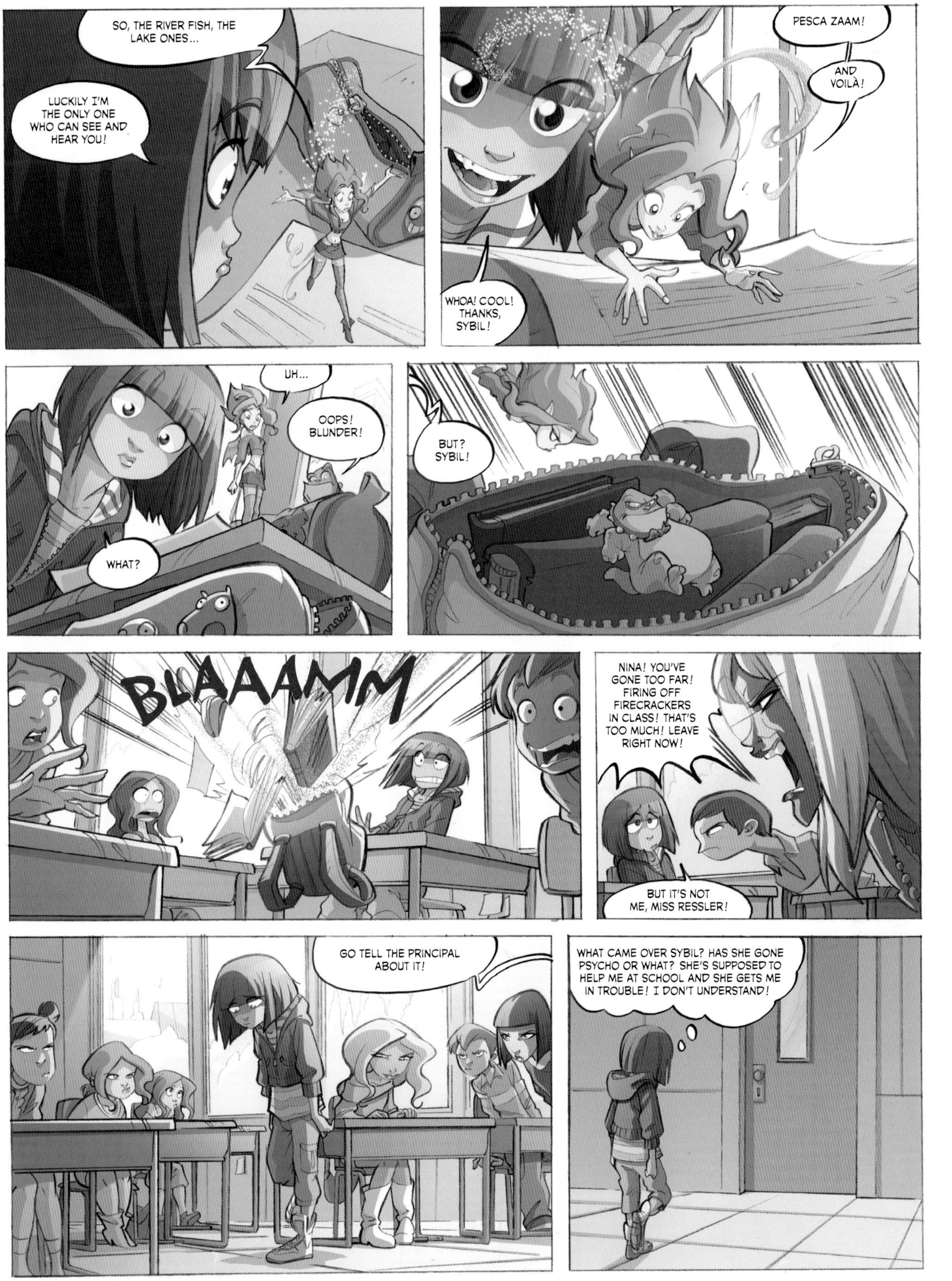
SO, THE RIVER FISH, THE LAKE ONES...
LUCKILY I'M THE ONLY ONE WHO CAN SEE AND HEAR YOU!
PESCA ZAAM!
AND VOILÀ!
WHOA! COOL! THANKS, SYBIL!
UH...
OOPS! BLUNDER!
WHAT?
BUT? SYBIL!
BLAAAMM
NINA! YOU'VE GONE TOO FAR! FIRING OFF FIRECRACKERS IN CLASS! THAT'S TOO MUCH! LEAVE RIGHT NOW!
BUT IT'S NOT ME, MISS RESSLER!
GO TELL THE PRINCIPAL ABOUT IT!
WHAT CAME OVER SYBIL? HAS SHE GONE PSYCHO OR WHAT? SHE'S SUPPOSED TO HELP ME AT SCHOOL AND SHE GETS ME IN TROUBLE! I DON'T UNDERSTAND!

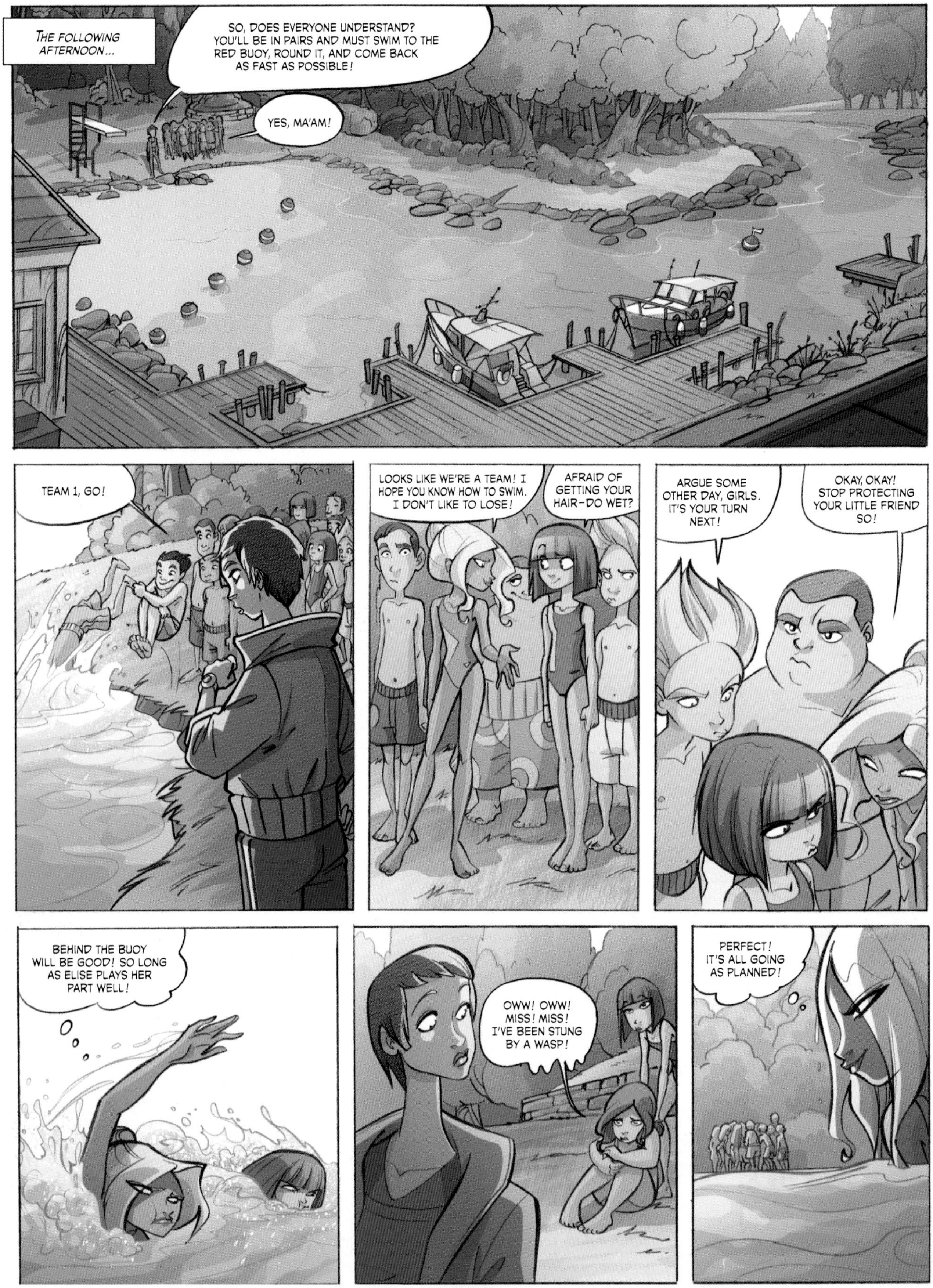
THE FOLLOWING AFTERNOON...
SO, DOES EVERYONE UNDERSTAND? YOU'LL BE IN PAIRS AND MUST SWIM TO THE RED BUOY, ROUND IT, AND COME BACK AS FAST AS POSSIBLE!
YES, MA'AM!
TEAM 1, GO!
LOOKS LIKE WE'RE A TEAM! I HOPE YOU KNOW HOW TO SWIM. I DON'T LIKE TO LOSE!
AFRAID OF GETTING YOUR HAIR-DO WET?
ARGUE SOME OTHER DAY, GIRLS. IT'S YOUR TURN NEXT!
OKAY, OKAY! STOP PROTECTING YOUR LITTLE FRIEND SO!
BEHIND THE BUOY WILL BE GOOD! SO LONG AS ELISE PLAYS HER PART WELL!
OWW! OWW! MISS! MISS! I'VE BEEN STUNG BY A WASP!
PERFECT! IT'S ALL GOING AS PLANNED!

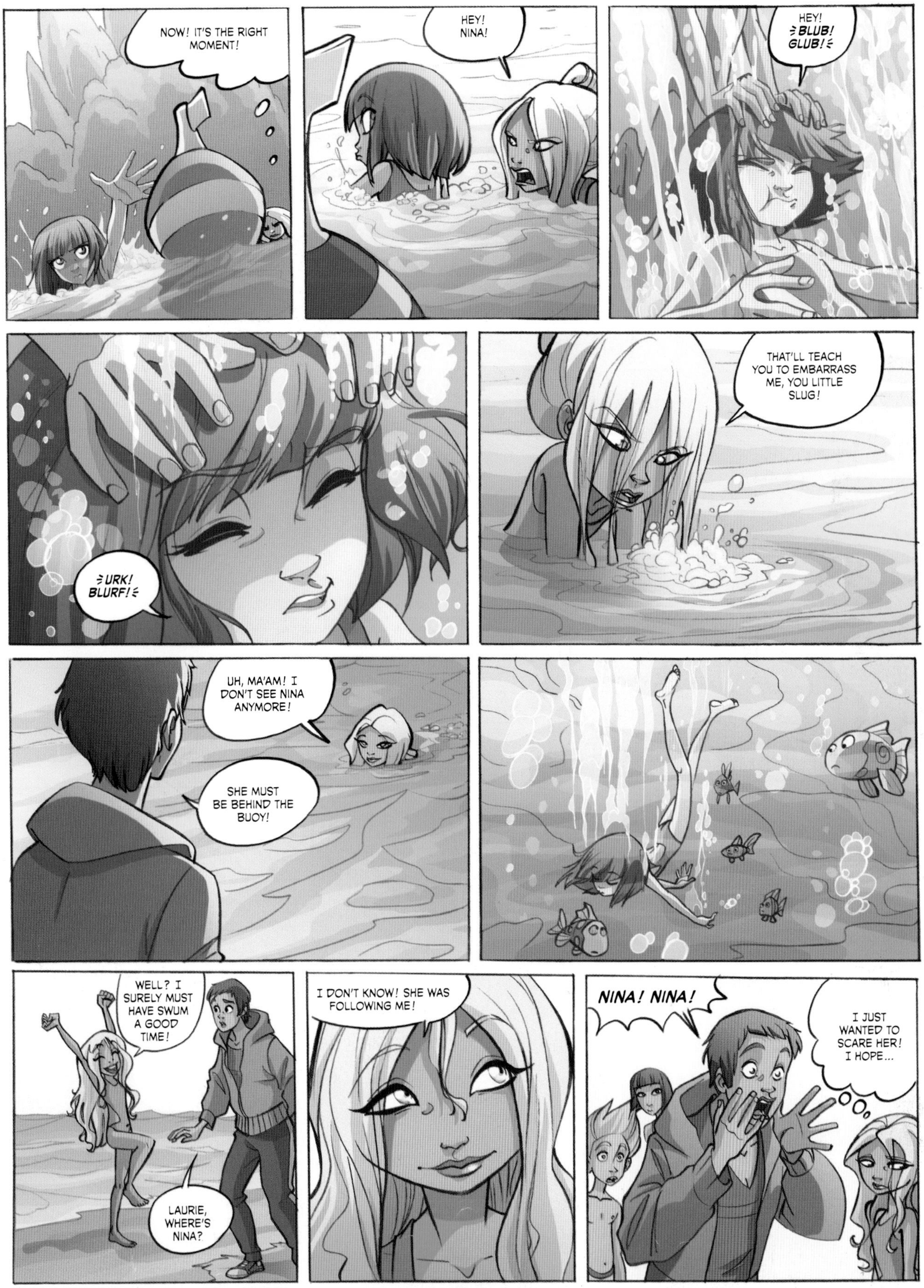
NOW! IT'S THE RIGHT MOMENT!
HEY! NINA!
HEY! BLUB! GLUB!
URK! BLURF!
THAT'LL TEACH YOU TO EMBARRASS ME, YOU LITTLE SLUG!
UH, MA'AM! I DON'T SEE NINA ANYMORE!
SHE MUST BE BEHIND THE BUOY!
WELL? I SURELY MUST HAVE SWUM A GOOD TIME!
LAURIE, WHERE'S NINA?
I DON'T KNOW! SHE WAS FOLLOWING ME!
NINA! NINA!
I JUST WANTED TO SCARE HER! I HOPE...

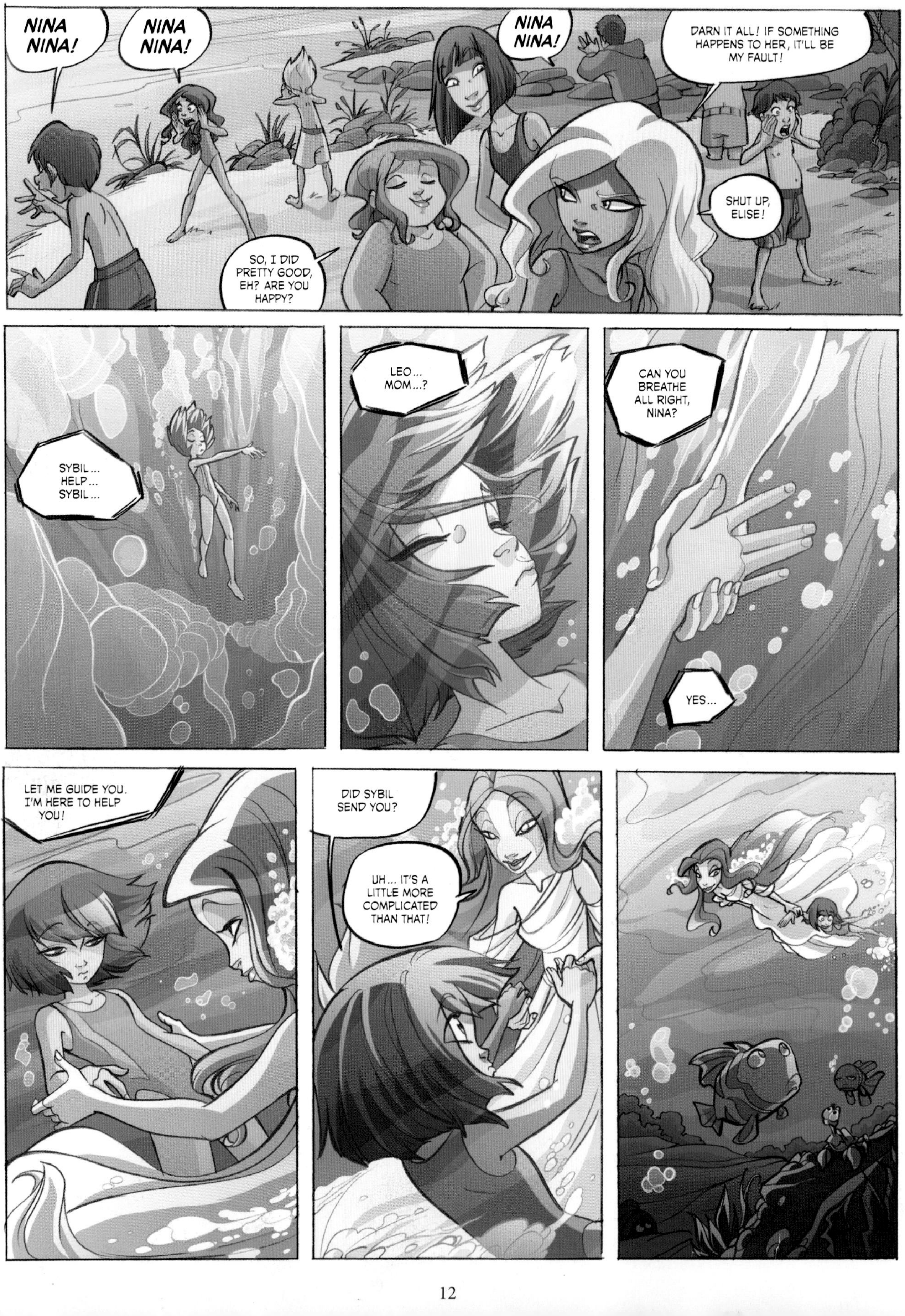
NINA NINA!
NINA NINA!
NINA NINA!
DARN IT ALL! IF SOMETHING HAPPENS TO HER, IT'LL BE MY FAULT!
SO, I DID PRETTY GOOD, EH? ARE YOU HAPPY?
SHUT UP, ELISE!
SYBIL... HELP... SYBIL...
LEO... MOM...?
CAN YOU BREATHE ALL RIGHT, NINA?
YES...
LET ME GUIDE YOU. I'M HERE TO HELP YOU!
DID SYBIL SEND YOU?
UH... IT'S A LITTLE MORE COMPLICATED THAN THAT!

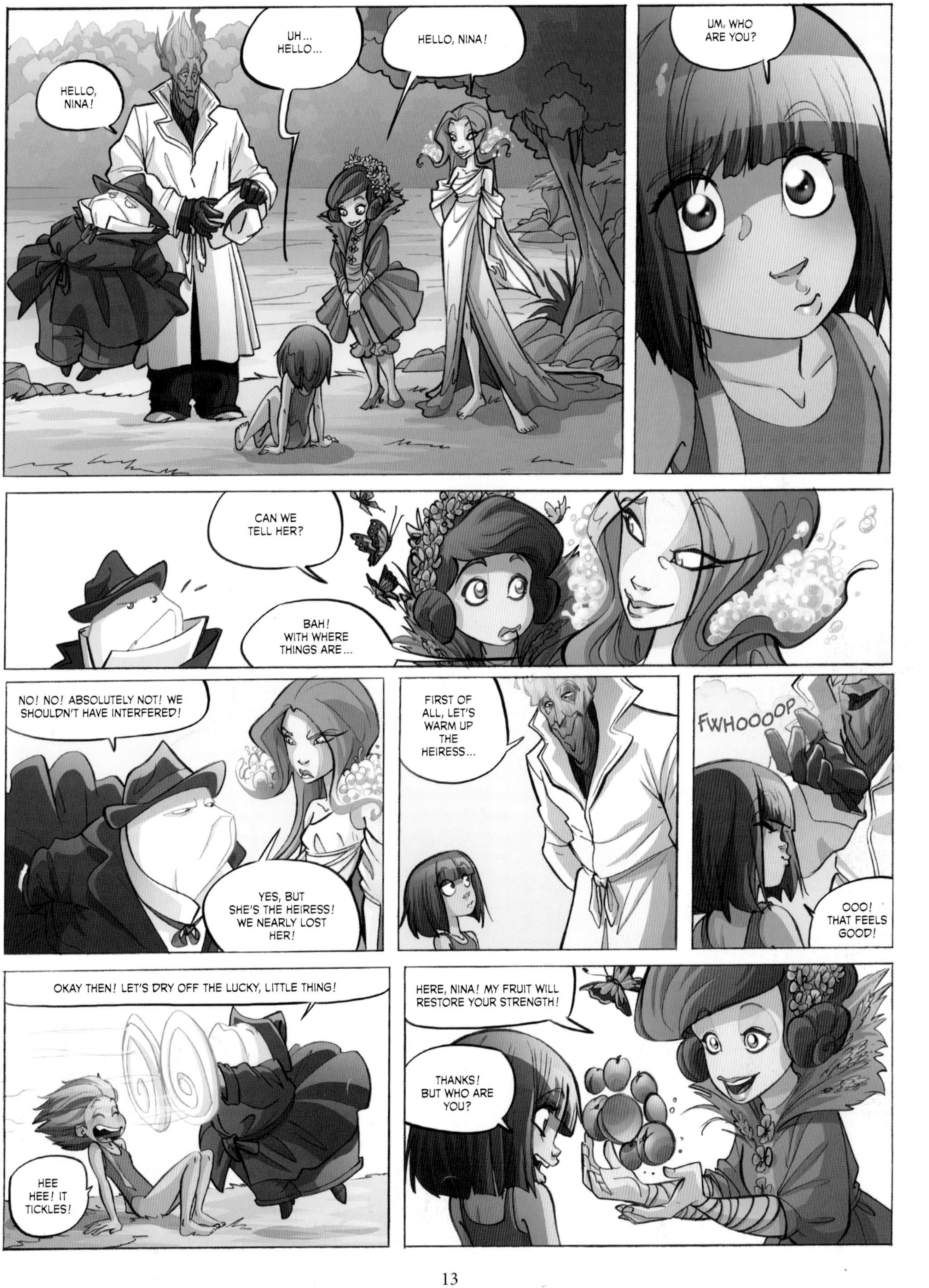
HELLO, NINA!
UH... HELLO...
HELLO, NINA!
UM, WHO ARE YOU?
CAN WE TELL HER?
BAH! WITH WHERE THINGS ARE...
NO! NO! ABSOLUTELY NOT! WE SHOULDN'T HAVE INTERFERED!
YES, BUT SHE'S THE HEIRESS! WE NEARLY LOST HER!
FIRST OF ALL, LET'S WARM UP THE HEIRESS...
FWHOOOOP
OOO! THAT FEELS GOOD!
OKAY THEN! LET'S DRY OFF THE LUCKY, LITTLE THING!
HEE HEE! IT TICKLES!
HERE, NINA! MY FRUIT WILL RESTORE YOUR STRENGTH!
THANKS! BUT WHO ARE YOU?

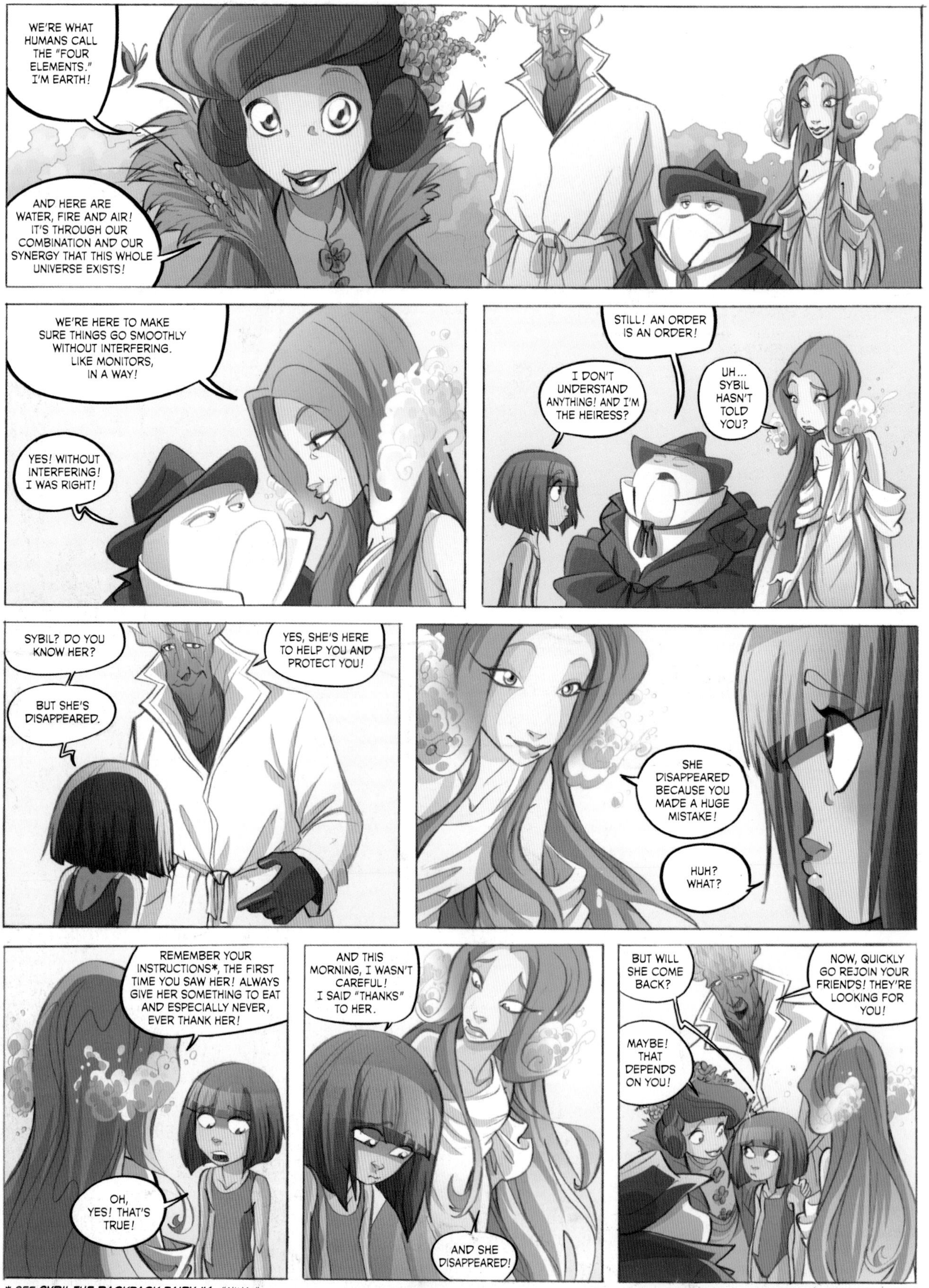
WE'RE WHAT HUMANS CALL THE "FOUR ELEMENTS." I'M EARTH!
AND HERE ARE WATER, FIRE AND AIR! IT'S THROUGH OUR COMBINATION AND OUR SYNERGY THAT THIS WHOLE UNIVERSE EXISTS!
WE'RE HERE TO MAKE SURE THINGS GO SMOOTHLY WITHOUT INTERFERING. LIKE MONITORS, IN A WAY!
YES! WITHOUT INTERFERING! I WAS RIGHT!
STILL! AN ORDER IS AN ORDER!
I DON'T UNDERSTAND ANYTHING! AND I'M THE HEIRESS?
UH... SYBIL HASN'T TOLD YOU?
SYBIL? DO YOU KNOW HER?
YES, SHE'S HERE TO HELP YOU AND PROTECT YOU!
BUT SHE'S DISAPPEARED.
SHE DISAPPEARED BECAUSE YOU MADE A HUGE MISTAKE!
HUH? WHAT?
REMEMBER YOUR INSTRUCTIONS*, THE FIRST TIME YOU SAW HER! ALWAYS GIVE HER SOMETHING TO EAT AND ESPECIALLY NEVER, EVER THANK HER!
OH, YES! THAT'S TRUE!
AND THIS MORNING, I WASN'T CAREFUL! I SAID "THANKS" TO HER.
AND SHE DISAPPEARED!
BUT WILL SHE COME BACK?
NOW, QUICKLY GO REJOIN YOUR FRIENDS! THEY'RE LOOKING FOR YOU!
MAYBE! THAT DEPENDS ON YOU!

* SEE **SYBIL THE BACKPACK FAIRY #1**: "NINA."

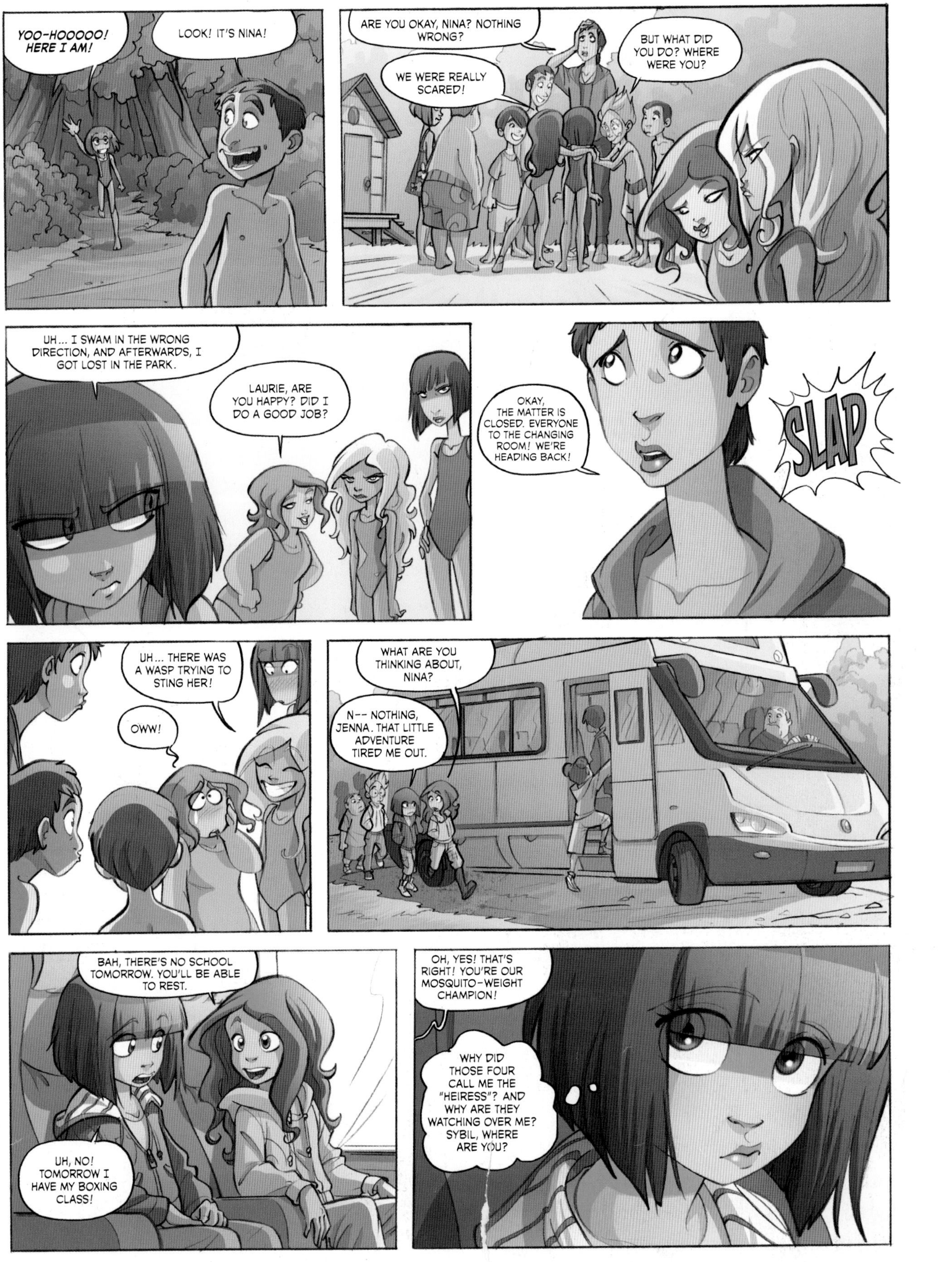
YOO-HOOOOO! HERE I AM!
LOOK! IT'S NINA!
ARE YOU OKAY, NINA? NOTHING WRONG?
WE WERE REALLY SCARED!
BUT WHAT DID YOU DO? WHERE WERE YOU?
UH... I SWAM IN THE WRONG DIRECTION, AND AFTERWARDS, I GOT LOST IN THE PARK.
LAURIE, ARE YOU HAPPY? DID I DO A GOOD JOB?
OKAY, THE MATTER IS CLOSED. EVERYONE TO THE CHANGING ROOM! WE'RE HEADING BACK!
SLAP
UH... THERE WAS A WASP TRYING TO STING HER!
OWW!
WHAT ARE YOU THINKING ABOUT, NINA?
N-- NOTHING, JENNA. THAT LITTLE ADVENTURE TIRED ME OUT.
BAH, THERE'S NO SCHOOL TOMORROW. YOU'LL BE ABLE TO REST.
UH, NO! TOMORROW I HAVE MY BOXING CLASS!
OH, YES! THAT'S RIGHT! YOU'RE OUR MOSQUITO-WEIGHT CHAMPION!
WHY DID THOSE FOUR CALL ME THE "HEIRESS"? AND WHY ARE THEY WATCHING OVER ME? SYBIL, WHERE ARE YOU?

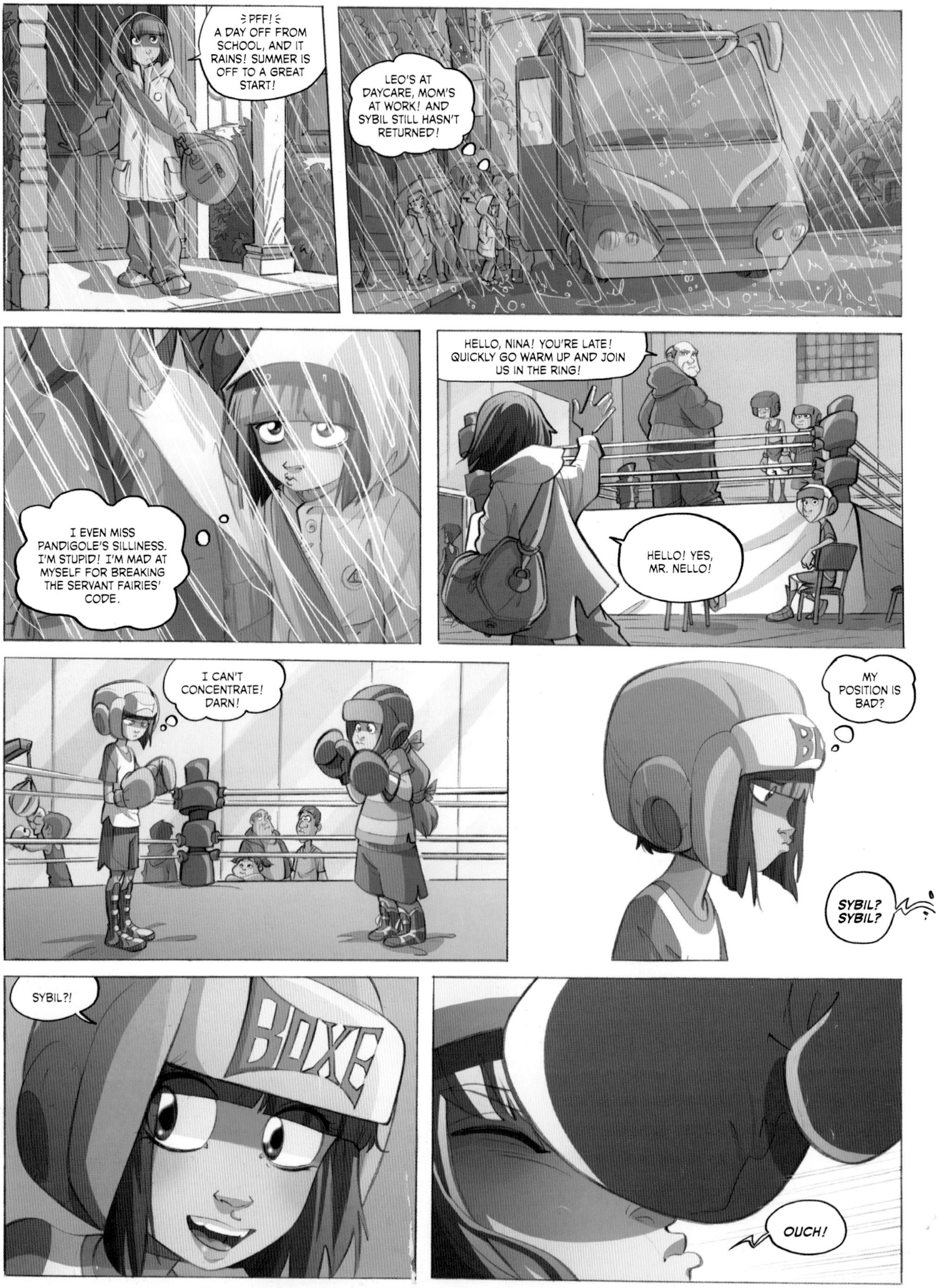
PFF!
A DAY OFF FROM SCHOOL, AND IT RAINS! SUMMER IS OFF TO A GREAT START!
LEO'S AT DAYCARE, MOM'S AT WORK! AND SYBIL STILL HASN'T RETURNED!
I EVEN MISS PANDIGOLE'S SILLINESS. I'M STUPID! I'M MAD AT MYSELF FOR BREAKING THE SERVANT FAIRIES' CODE.
HELLO, NINA! YOU'RE LATE! QUICKLY GO WARM UP AND JOIN US IN THE RING!
HELLO! YES, MR. NELLO!
I CAN'T CONCENTRATE! DARN!
MY POSITION IS BAD?
SYBIL? SYBIL?
SYBIL?!
BOXE
OUCH!

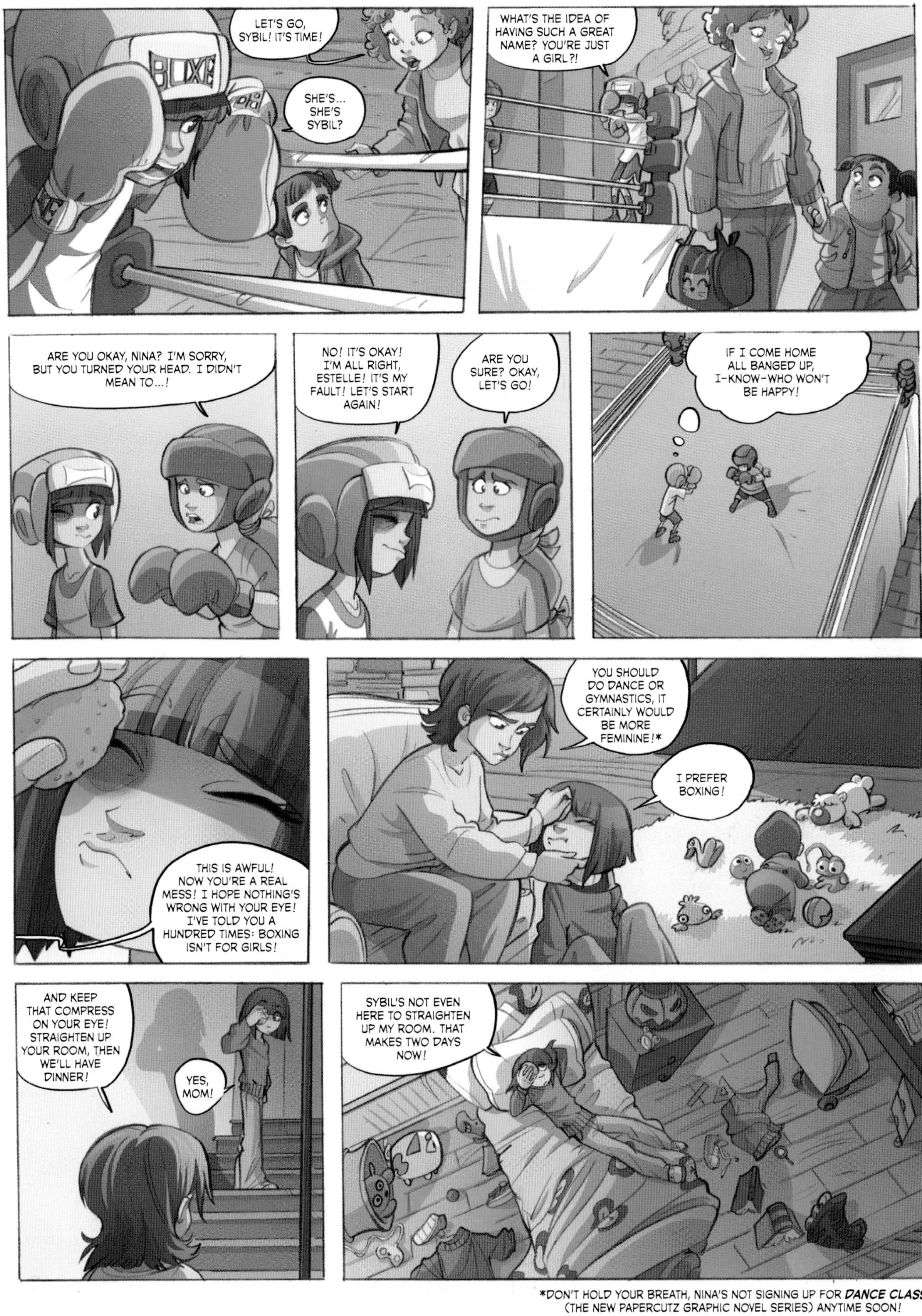
LET'S GO, SYBIL! IT'S TIME!
BOXE
SHE'S... SHE'S SYBIL?
WHAT'S THE IDEA OF HAVING SUCH A GREAT NAME? YOU'RE JUST A GIRL?!
ARE YOU OKAY, NINA? I'M SORRY, BUT YOU TURNED YOUR HEAD. I DIDN'T MEAN TO...!
NO! IT'S OKAY! I'M ALL RIGHT, ESTELLE! IT'S MY FAULT! LET'S START AGAIN!
ARE YOU SURE? OKAY, LET'S GO!
IF I COME HOME ALL BANGED UP, I-KNOW-WHO WON'T BE HAPPY!
THIS IS AWFUL! NOW YOU'RE A REAL MESS! I HOPE NOTHING'S WRONG WITH YOUR EYE! I'VE TOLD YOU A HUNDRED TIMES: BOXING ISN'T FOR GIRLS!
YOU SHOULD DO DANCE OR GYMNASTICS, IT CERTAINLY WOULD BE MORE FEMININE!*
I PREFER BOXING!
AND KEEP THAT COMPRESS ON YOUR EYE! STRAIGHTEN UP YOUR ROOM, THEN WE'LL HAVE DINNER!
YES, MOM!
SYBIL'S NOT EVEN HERE TO STRAIGHTEN UP MY ROOM. THAT MAKES TWO DAYS NOW!

*DON'T HOLD YOUR BREATH, NINA'S NOT SIGNING UP FOR ***DANCE CLASS*** (THE NEW PAPERCUTZ GRAPHIC NOVEL SERIES) ANYTIME SOON!

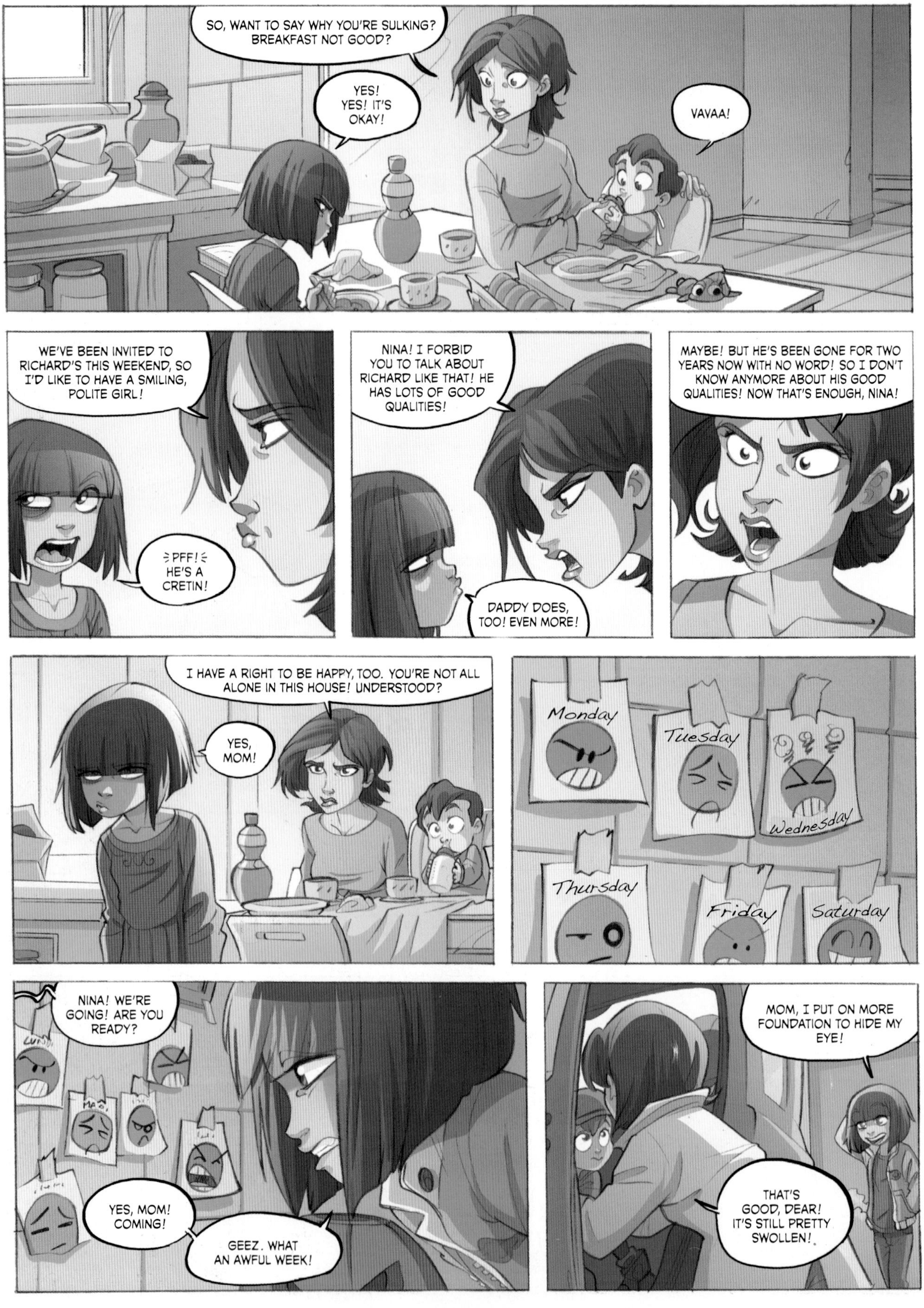

SO, WANT TO SAY WHY YOU'RE SULKING? BREAKFAST NOT GOOD?
YES! YES! IT'S OKAY!
VAVAA!
WE'VE BEEN INVITED TO RICHARD'S THIS WEEKEND, SO I'D LIKE TO HAVE A SMILING, POLITE GIRL!
PFF! HE'S A CRETIN!
NINA! I FORBID YOU TO TALK ABOUT RICHARD LIKE THAT! HE HAS LOTS OF GOOD QUALITIES!
DADDY DOES, TOO! EVEN MORE!
MAYBE! BUT HE'S BEEN GONE FOR TWO YEARS NOW WITH NO WORD! SO I DON'T KNOW ANYMORE ABOUT HIS GOOD QUALITIES! NOW THAT'S ENOUGH, NINA!
I HAVE A RIGHT TO BE HAPPY, TOO. YOU'RE NOT ALL ALONE IN THIS HOUSE! UNDERSTOOD?
YES, MOM!
Monday
Tuesday
Wednesday
Thursday
Friday
Saturday
NINA! WE'RE GOING! ARE YOU READY?
YES, MOM! COMING!
GEEZ. WHAT AN AWFUL WEEK!
MOM, I PUT ON MORE FOUNDATION TO HIDE MY EYE!
THAT'S GOOD, DEAR! IT'S STILL PRETTY SWOLLEN!

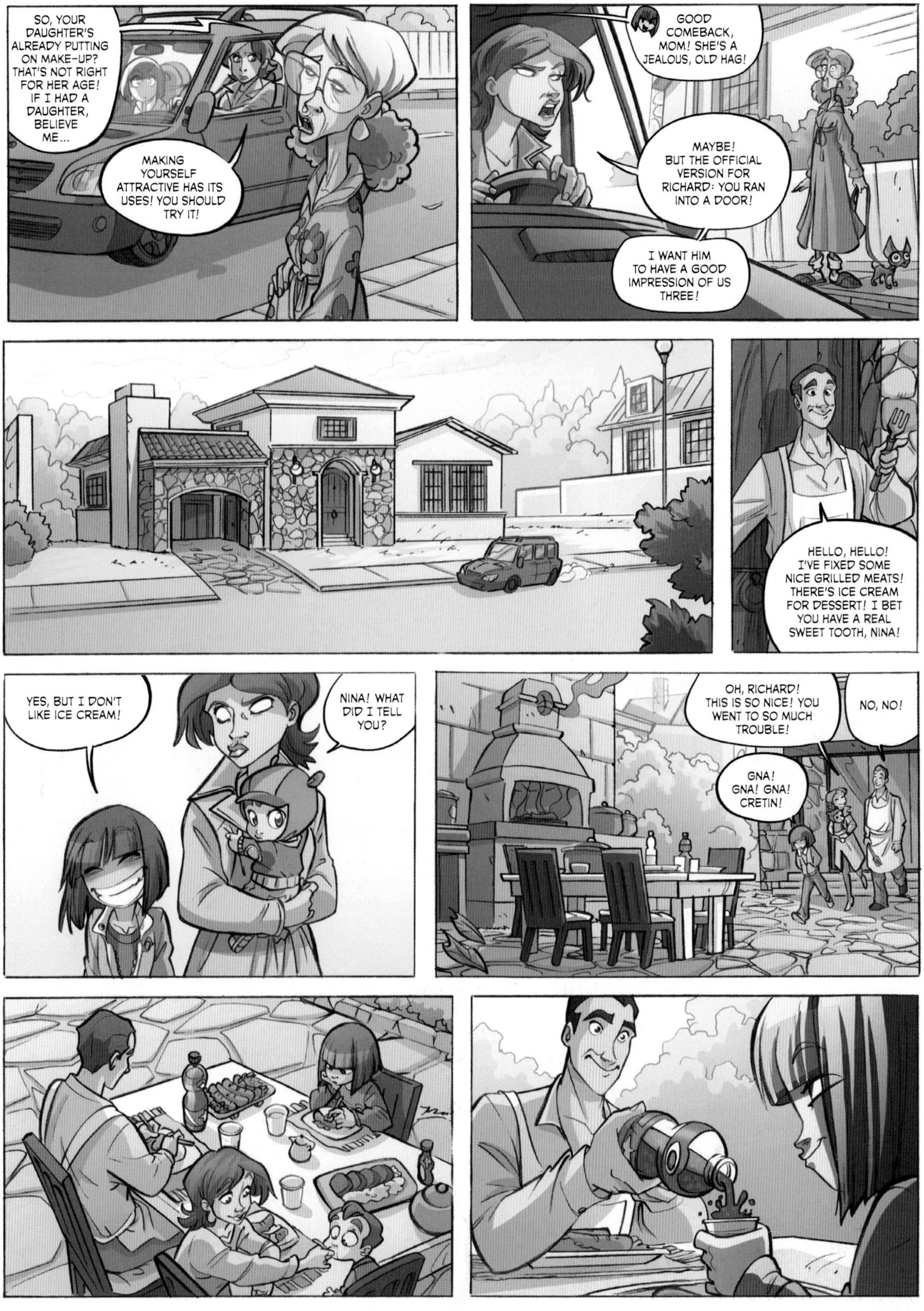
SO, YOUR DAUGHTER'S ALREADY PUTTING ON MAKE-UP? THAT'S NOT RIGHT FOR HER AGE! IF I HAD A DAUGHTER, BELIEVE ME...
MAKING YOURSELF ATTRACTIVE HAS ITS USES! YOU SHOULD TRY IT!
GOOD COMEBACK, MOM! SHE'S A JEALOUS, OLD HAG!
MAYBE! BUT THE OFFICIAL VERSION FOR RICHARD: YOU RAN INTO A DOOR!
I WANT HIM TO HAVE A GOOD IMPRESSION OF US THREE!
HELLO, HELLO! I'VE FIXED SOME NICE GRILLED MEATS! THERE'S ICE CREAM FOR DESSERT! I BET YOU HAVE A REAL SWEET TOOTH, NINA!
YES, BUT I DON'T LIKE ICE CREAM!
NINA! WHAT DID I TELL YOU?
OH, RICHARD! THIS IS SO NICE! YOU WENT TO SO MUCH TROUBLE!
NO, NO!
GNA! GNA! GNA! CRETIN!

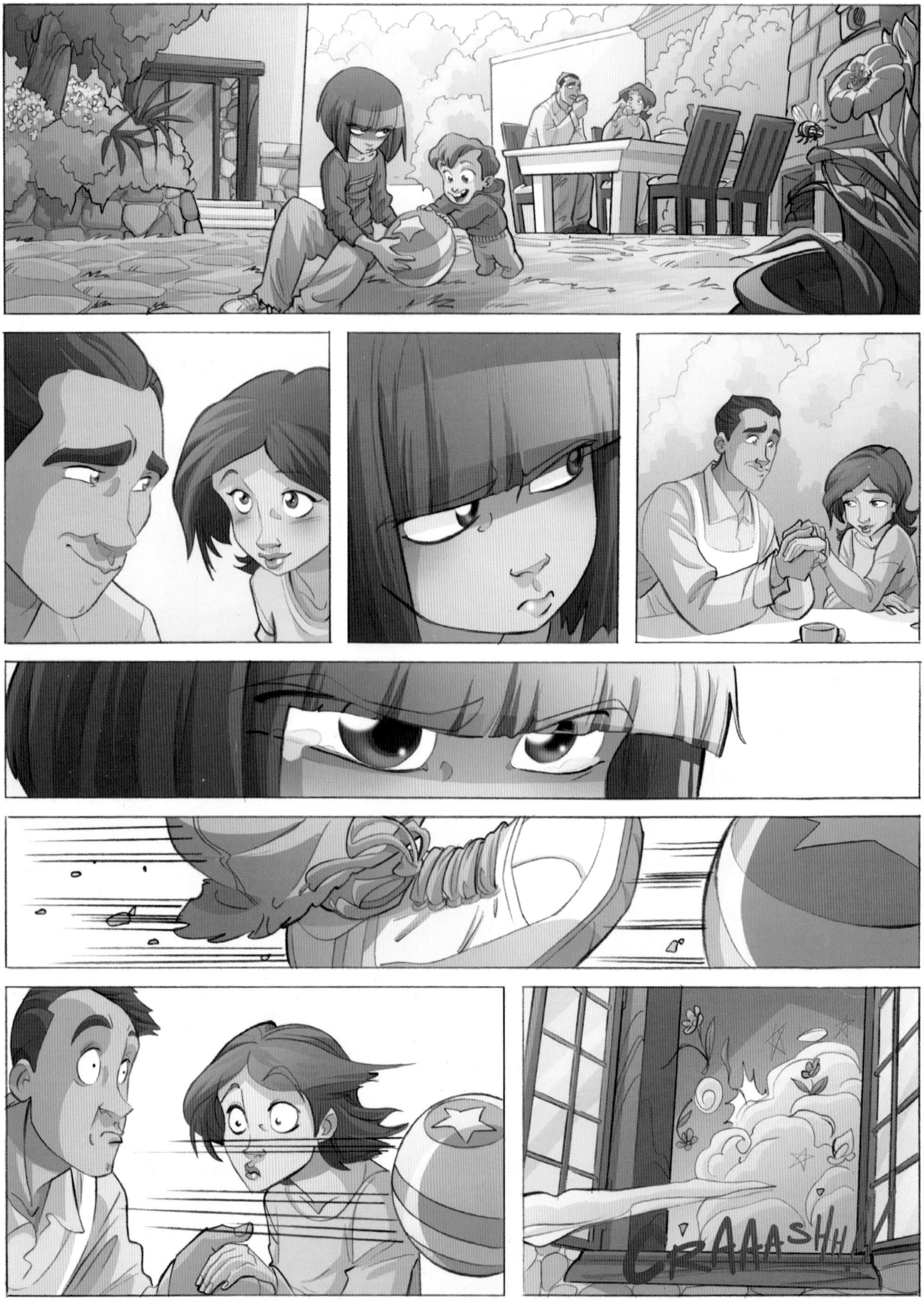
CRAAASHH

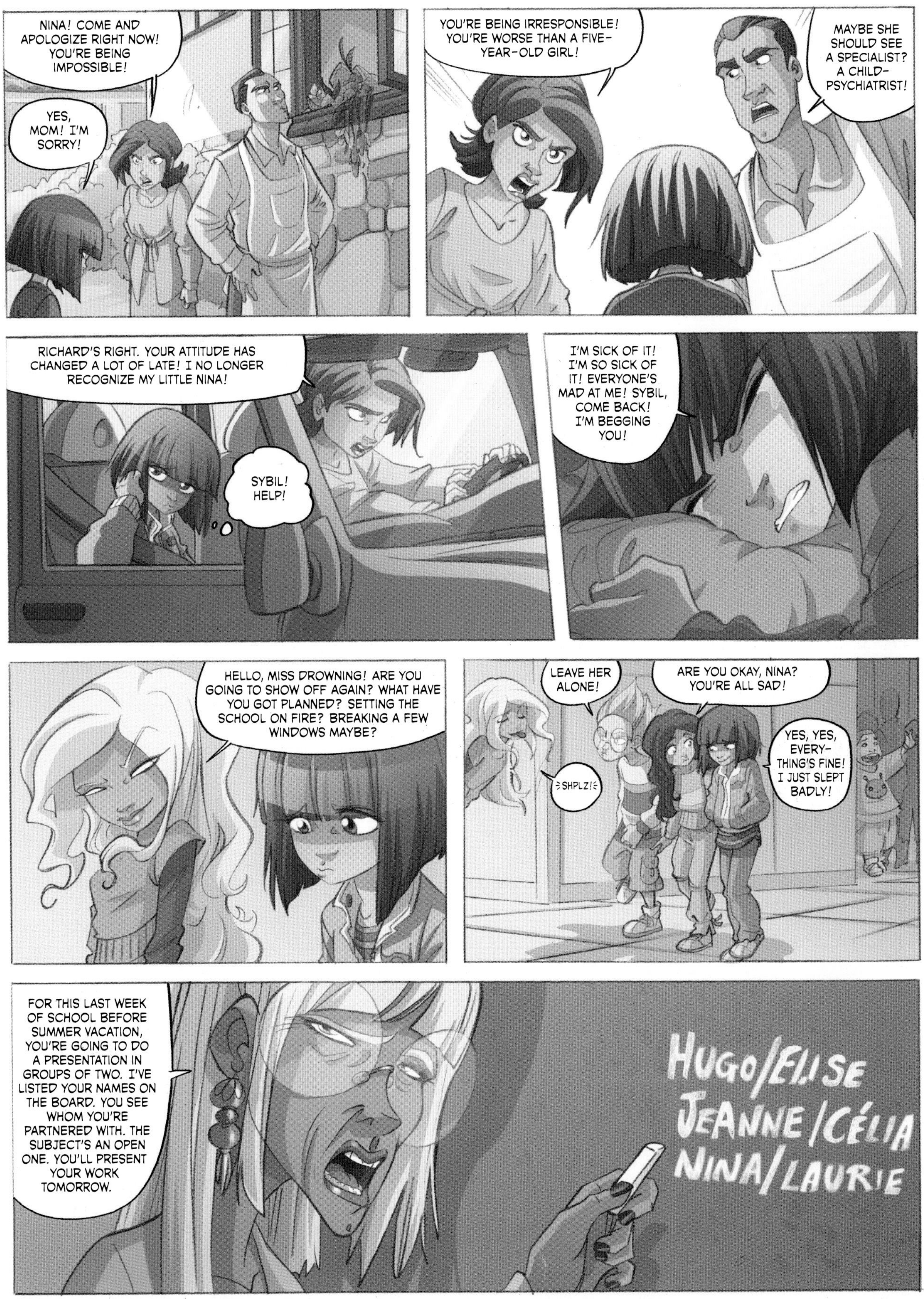
NINA! COME AND APOLOGIZE RIGHT NOW! YOU'RE BEING IMPOSSIBLE!
YES, MOM! I'M SORRY!
YOU'RE BEING IRRESPONSIBLE! YOU'RE WORSE THAN A FIVE-YEAR-OLD GIRL!
MAYBE SHE SHOULD SEE A SPECIALIST? A CHILD-PSYCHIATRIST!
RICHARD'S RIGHT. YOUR ATTITUDE HAS CHANGED A LOT OF LATE! I NO LONGER RECOGNIZE MY LITTLE NINA!
SYBIL! HELP!
I'M SICK OF IT! I'M SO SICK OF IT! EVERYONE'S MAD AT ME! SYBIL, COME BACK! I'M BEGGING YOU!
HELLO, MISS DROWNING! ARE YOU GOING TO SHOW OFF AGAIN? WHAT HAVE YOU GOT PLANNED? SETTING THE SCHOOL ON FIRE? BREAKING A FEW WINDOWS MAYBE?
LEAVE HER ALONE!
ARE YOU OKAY, NINA? YOU'RE ALL SAD!
SHPLZ!
YES, YES, EVERYTHING'S FINE! I JUST SLEPT BADLY!
FOR THIS LAST WEEK OF SCHOOL BEFORE SUMMER VACATION, YOU'RE GOING TO DO A PRESENTATION IN GROUPS OF TWO. I'VE LISTED YOUR NAMES ON THE BOARD. YOU SEE WHOM YOU'RE PARTNERED WITH. THE SUBJECT'S AN OPEN ONE. YOU'LL PRESENT YOUR WORK TOMORROW.
HUGO/ELISE
JEANNE/CÉLIA
NINA/LAURIE

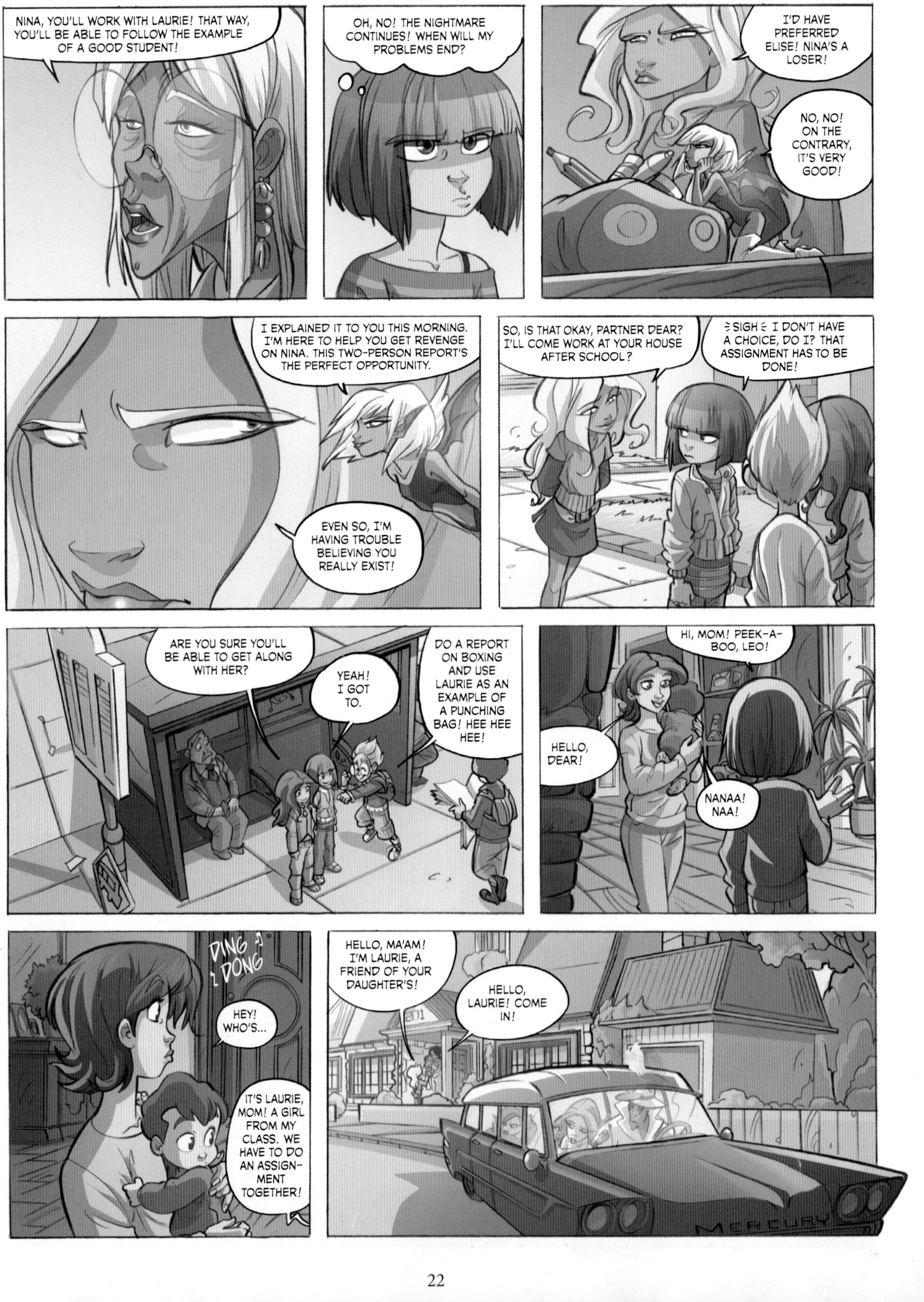
NINA, YOU'LL WORK WITH LAURIE! THAT WAY, YOU'LL BE ABLE TO FOLLOW THE EXAMPLE OF A GOOD STUDENT!
OH, NO! THE NIGHTMARE CONTINUES! WHEN WILL MY PROBLEMS END?
I'D HAVE PREFERRED ELISE! NINA'S A LOSER!
NO, NO! ON THE CONTRARY, IT'S VERY GOOD!
I EXPLAINED IT TO YOU THIS MORNING. I'M HERE TO HELP YOU GET REVENGE ON NINA. THIS TWO-PERSON REPORT'S THE PERFECT OPPORTUNITY.
EVEN SO, I'M HAVING TROUBLE BELIEVING YOU REALLY EXIST!
SO, IS THAT OKAY, PARTNER DEAR? I'LL COME WORK AT YOUR HOUSE AFTER SCHOOL?
SIGH I DON'T HAVE A CHOICE, DO I? THAT ASSIGNMENT HAS TO BE DONE!
ARE YOU SURE YOU'LL BE ABLE TO GET ALONG WITH HER?
YEAH! I GOT TO.
DO A REPORT ON BOXING AND USE LAURIE AS AN EXAMPLE OF A PUNCHING BAG! HEE HEE HEE!
HI, MOM! PEEK-A-BOO, LEO!
HELLO, DEAR!
NANAA! NAA!
DING DONG
HEY! WHO'S...
IT'S LAURIE, MOM! A GIRL FROM MY CLASS. WE HAVE TO DO AN ASSIGNMENT TOGETHER!
HELLO, MA'AM! I'M LAURIE, A FRIEND OF YOUR DAUGHTER'S!
HELLO, LAURIE! COME IN!
MERCURY

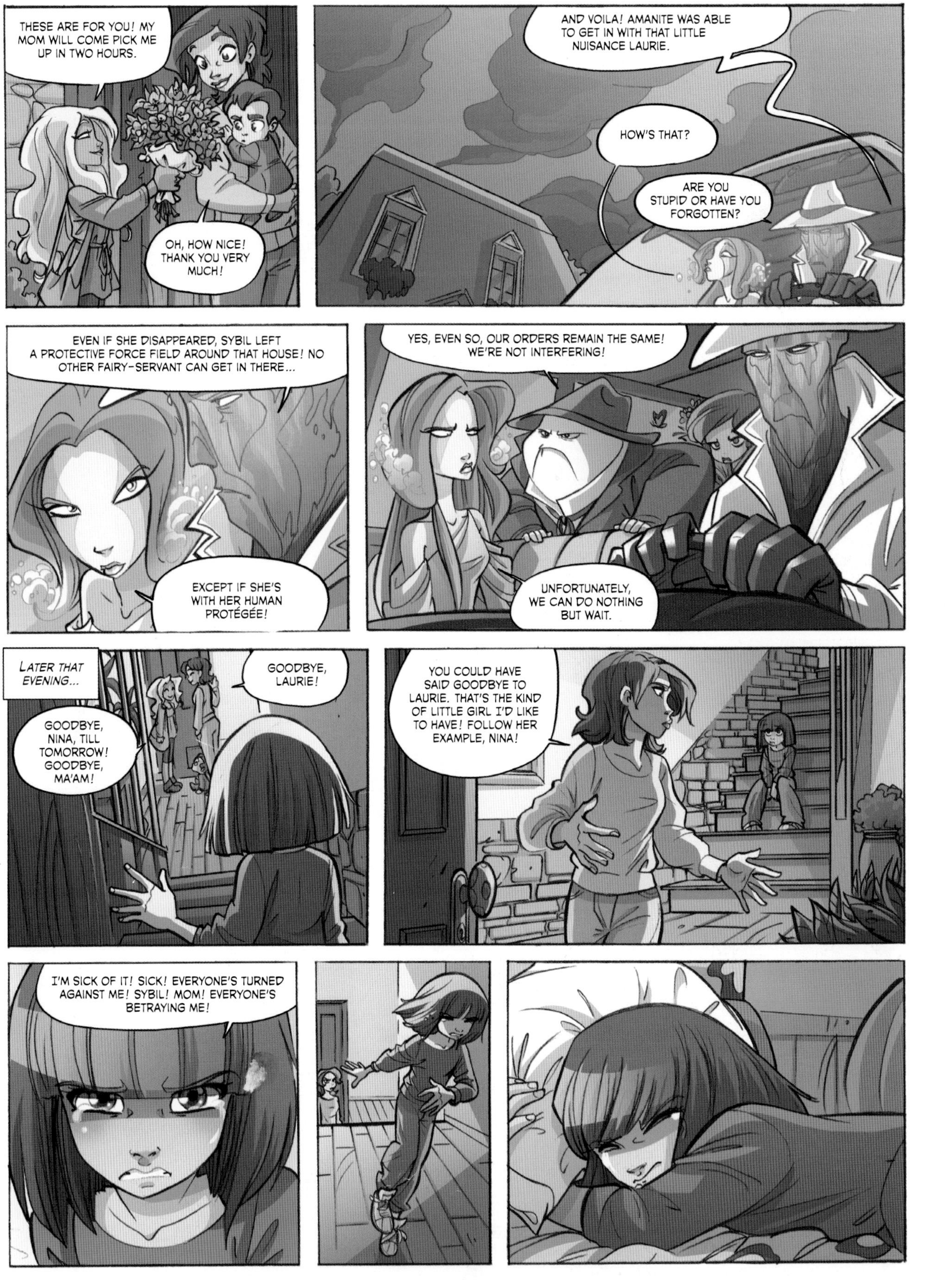
THESE ARE FOR YOU! MY MOM WILL COME PICK ME UP IN TWO HOURS.
OH, HOW NICE! THANK YOU VERY MUCH!
AND VOILA! AMANITE WAS ABLE TO GET IN WITH THAT LITTLE NUISANCE LAURIE.
HOW'S THAT?
ARE YOU STUPID OR HAVE YOU FORGOTTEN?
EVEN IF SHE DISAPPEARED, SYBIL LEFT A PROTECTIVE FORCE FIELD AROUND THAT HOUSE! NO OTHER FAIRY-SERVANT CAN GET IN THERE...
EXCEPT IF SHE'S WITH HER HUMAN PROTÉGÉE!
YES, EVEN SO, OUR ORDERS REMAIN THE SAME! WE'RE NOT INTERFERING!
UNFORTUNATELY, WE CAN DO NOTHING BUT WAIT.
LATER THAT EVENING...
GOODBYE, LAURIE!
GOODBYE, NINA, TILL TOMORROW! GOODBYE, MA'AM!
YOU COULD HAVE SAID GOODBYE TO LAURIE. THAT'S THE KIND OF LITTLE GIRL I'D LIKE TO HAVE! FOLLOW HER EXAMPLE, NINA!
I'M SICK OF IT! SICK! EVERYONE'S TURNED AGAINST ME! SYBIL! MOM! EVERYONE'S BETRAYING ME!

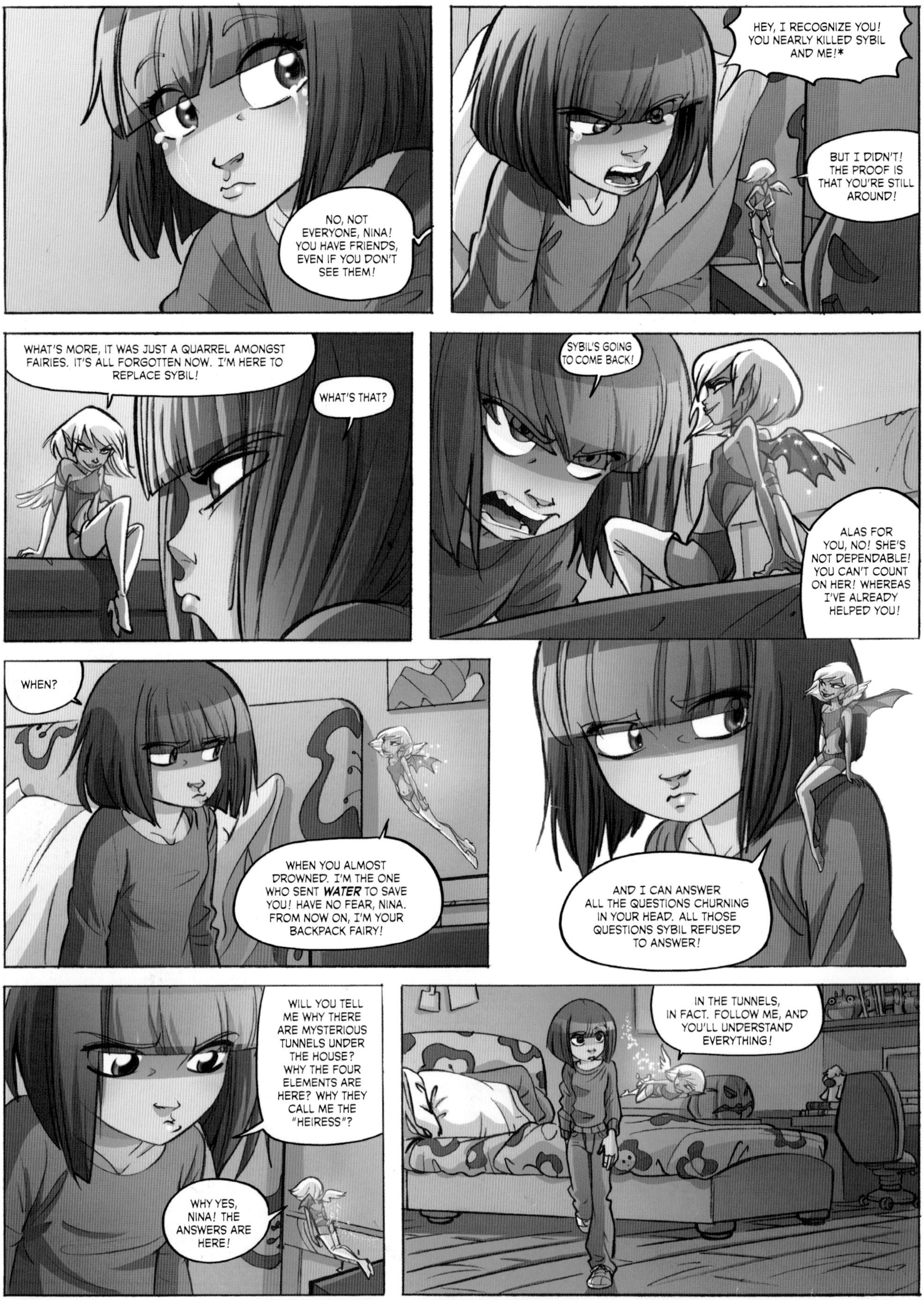
NO, NOT EVERYONE, NINA! YOU HAVE FRIENDS, EVEN IF YOU DON'T SEE THEM!
HEY, I RECOGNIZE YOU! YOU NEARLY KILLED SYBIL AND ME!*
BUT I DIDN'T! THE PROOF IS THAT YOU'RE STILL AROUND!
WHAT'S MORE, IT WAS JUST A QUARREL AMONGST FAIRIES. IT'S ALL FORGOTTEN NOW. I'M HERE TO REPLACE SYBIL!
WHAT'S THAT?
SYBIL'S GOING TO COME BACK!
ALAS FOR YOU, NO! SHE'S NOT DEPENDABLE! YOU CAN'T COUNT ON HER! WHEREAS I'VE ALREADY HELPED YOU!
WHEN?
WHEN YOU ALMOST DROWNED. I'M THE ONE WHO SENT **WATER** TO SAVE YOU! HAVE NO FEAR, NINA. FROM NOW ON, I'M YOUR BACKPACK FAIRY!
AND I CAN ANSWER ALL THE QUESTIONS CHURNING IN YOUR HEAD. ALL THOSE QUESTIONS SYBIL REFUSED TO ANSWER!
WILL YOU TELL ME WHY THERE ARE MYSTERIOUS TUNNELS UNDER THE HOUSE? WHY THE FOUR ELEMENTS ARE HERE? WHY THEY CALL ME THE "HEIRESS"?
WHY YES, NINA! THE ANSWERS ARE HERE!
IN THE TUNNELS, IN FACT. FOLLOW ME, AND YOU'LL UNDERSTAND EVERYTHING!

* *SEE **SYBIL THE BACKPACK FAIRY #1**: "NINA."*

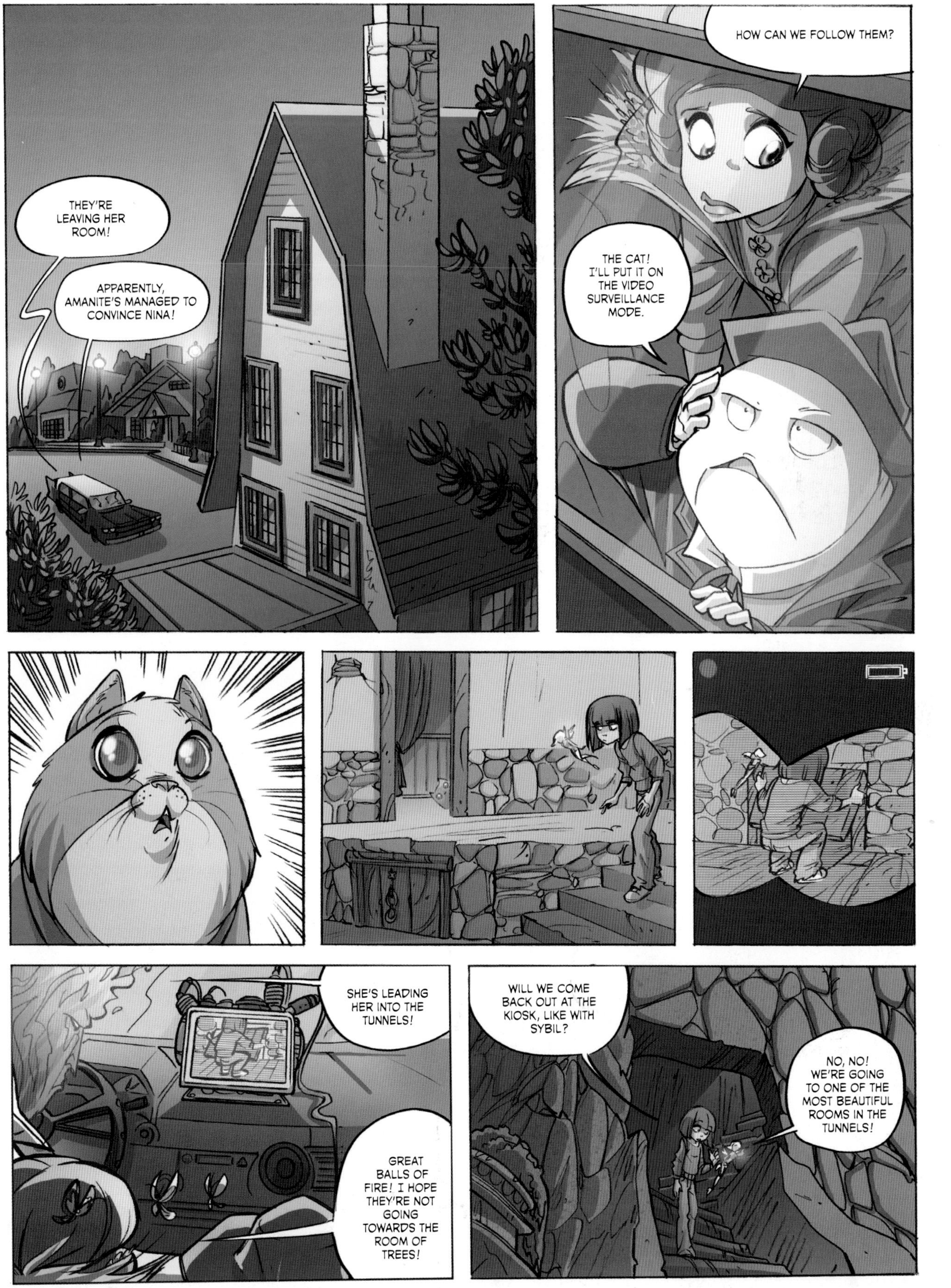
THEY'RE LEAVING HER ROOM!
APPARENTLY, AMANITE'S MANAGED TO CONVINCE NINA!
HOW CAN WE FOLLOW THEM?
THE CAT! I'LL PUT IT ON THE VIDEO SURVEILLANCE MODE.
SHE'S LEADING HER INTO THE TUNNELS!
GREAT BALLS OF FIRE! I HOPE THEY'RE NOT GOING TOWARDS THE ROOM OF TREES!
WILL WE COME BACK OUT AT THE KIOSK, LIKE WITH SYBIL?
NO, NO! WE'RE GOING TO ONE OF THE MOST BEAUTIFUL ROOMS IN THE TUNNELS!

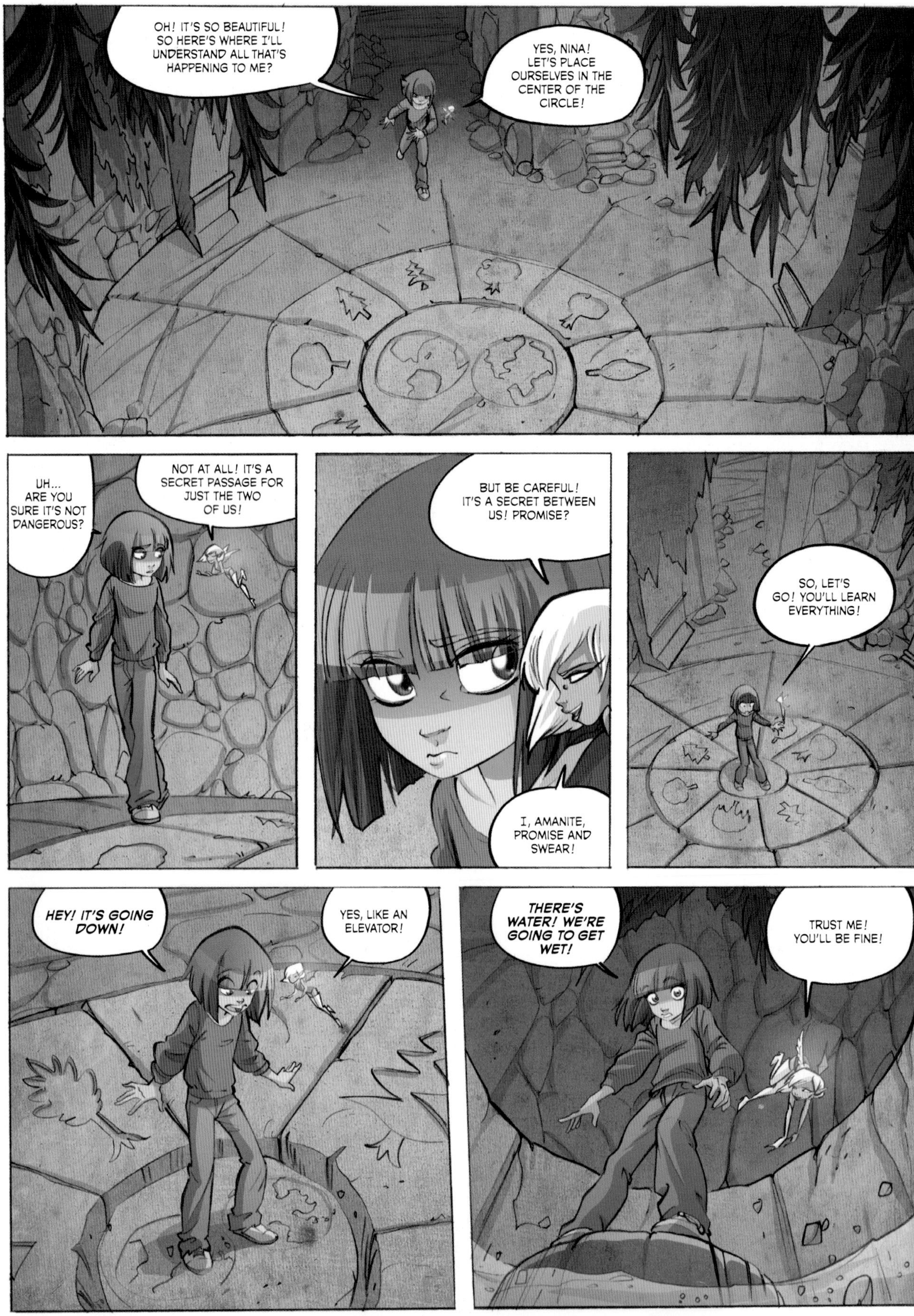
OH! IT'S SO BEAUTIFUL! SO HERE'S WHERE I'LL UNDERSTAND ALL THAT'S HAPPENING TO ME?
YES, NINA! LET'S PLACE OURSELVES IN THE CENTER OF THE CIRCLE!
UH... ARE YOU SURE IT'S NOT DANGEROUS?
NOT AT ALL! IT'S A SECRET PASSAGE FOR JUST THE TWO OF US!
BUT BE CAREFUL! IT'S A SECRET BETWEEN US! PROMISE?
I, AMANITE, PROMISE AND SWEAR!
SO, LET'S GO! YOU'LL LEARN EVERYTHING!
HEY! IT'S GOING DOWN!
YES, LIKE AN ELEVATOR!
THERE'S WATER! WE'RE GOING TO GET WET!
TRUST ME! YOU'LL BE FINE!

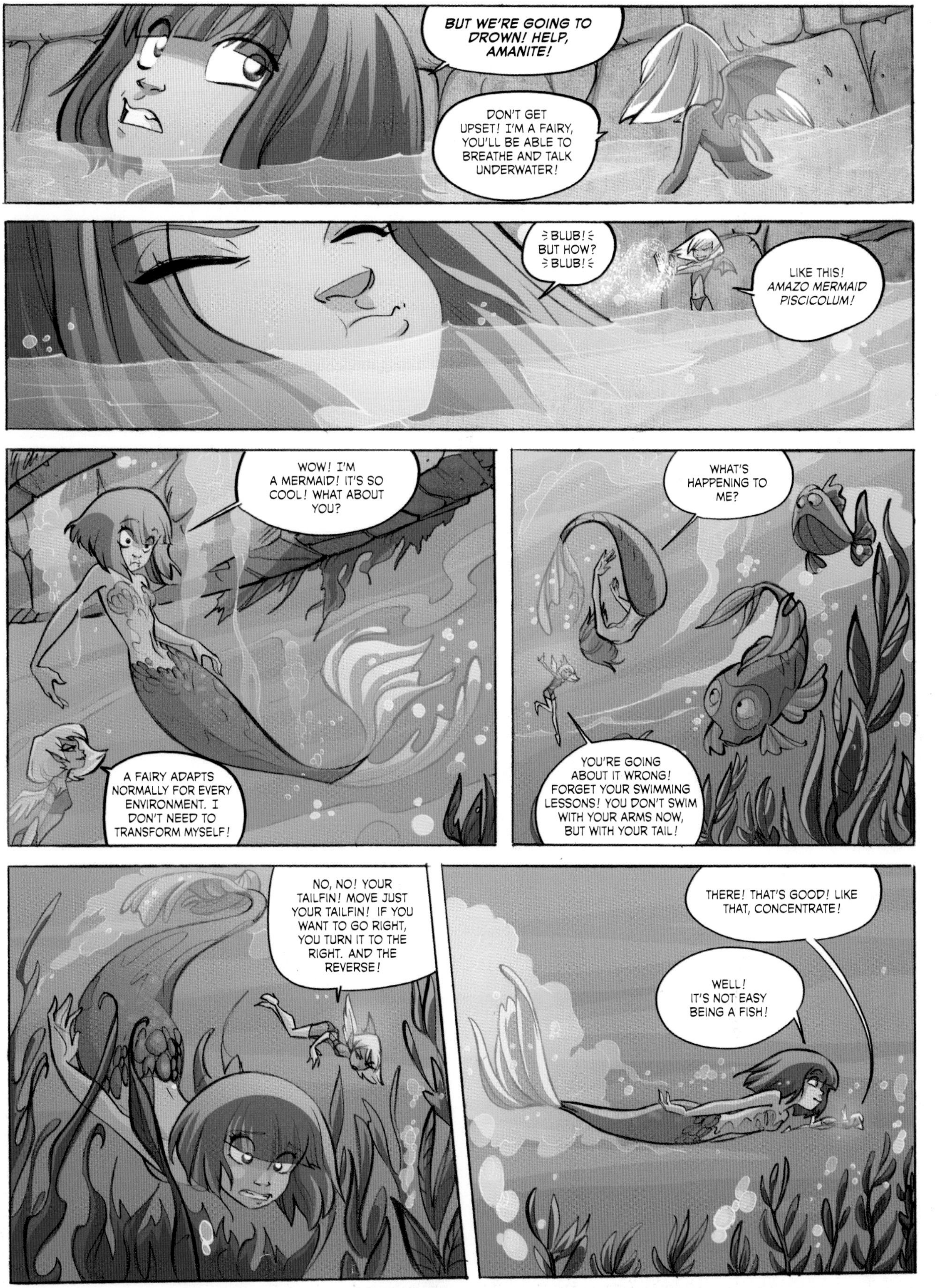
BUT WE'RE GOING TO DROWN! HELP, AMANITE!
DON'T GET UPSET! I'M A FAIRY, YOU'LL BE ABLE TO BREATHE AND TALK UNDERWATER!
BLUB! BUT HOW? BLUB!
LIKE THIS! AMAZO MERMAID PISCICOLUM!
WOW! I'M A MERMAID! IT'S SO COOL! WHAT ABOUT YOU?
A FAIRY ADAPTS NORMALLY FOR EVERY ENVIRONMENT. I DON'T NEED TO TRANSFORM MYSELF!
WHAT'S HAPPENING TO ME?
YOU'RE GOING ABOUT IT WRONG! FORGET YOUR SWIMMING LESSONS! YOU DON'T SWIM WITH YOUR ARMS NOW, BUT WITH YOUR TAIL!
NO, NO! YOUR TAILFIN! MOVE JUST YOUR TAILFIN! IF YOU WANT TO GO RIGHT, YOU TURN IT TO THE RIGHT. AND THE REVERSE!
THERE! THAT'S GOOD! LIKE THAT, CONCENTRATE!
WELL! IT'S NOT EASY BEING A FISH!

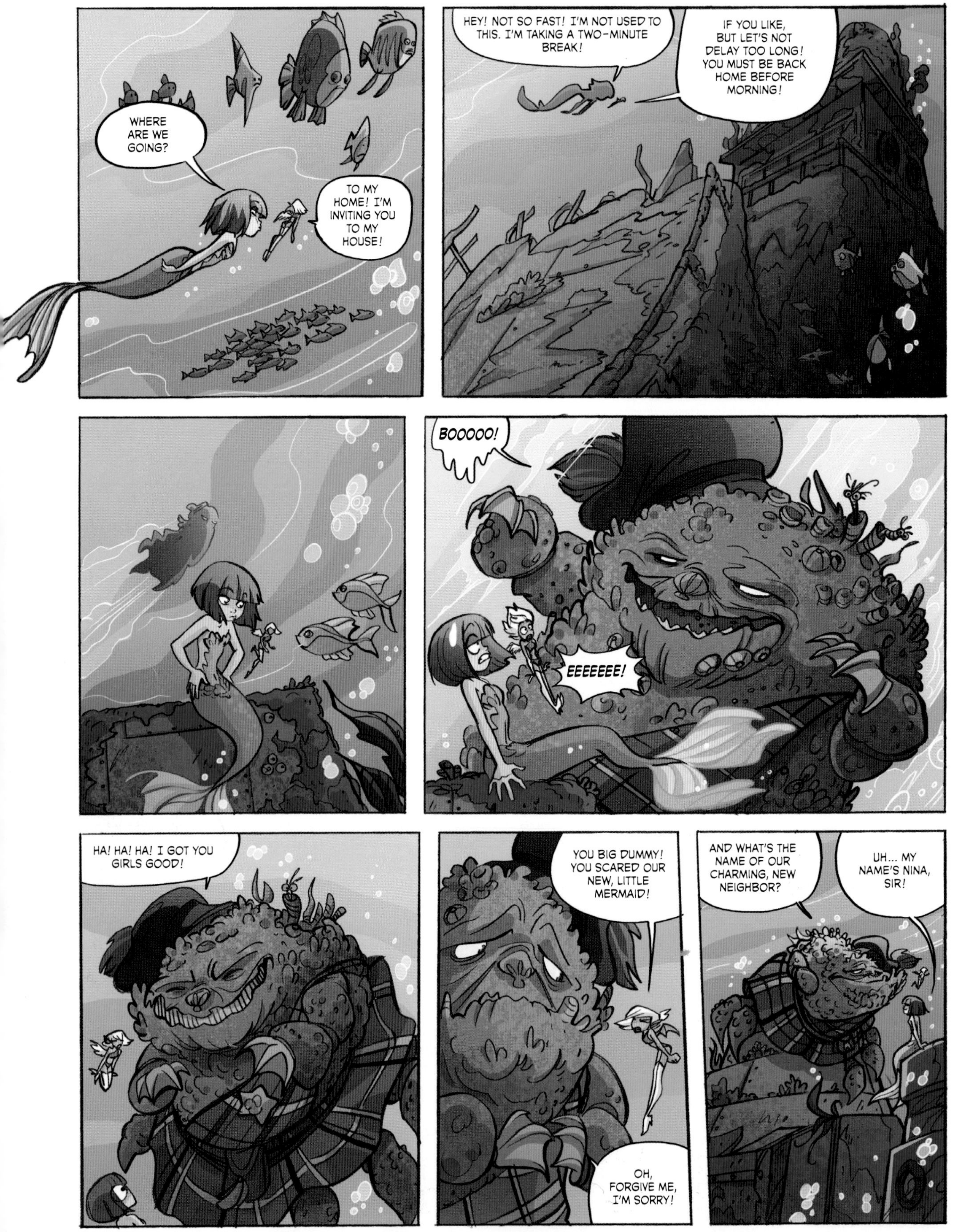
WHERE ARE WE GOING?
TO MY HOME! I'M INVITING YOU TO MY HOUSE!
HEY! NOT SO FAST! I'M NOT USED TO THIS. I'M TAKING A TWO-MINUTE BREAK!
IF YOU LIKE, BUT LET'S NOT DELAY TOO LONG! YOU MUST BE BACK HOME BEFORE MORNING!
BOOOOO!
EEEEEEE!
HA! HA! HA! I GOT YOU GIRLS GOOD!
YOU BIG DUMMY! YOU SCARED OUR NEW, LITTLE MERMAID!
OH, FORGIVE ME, I'M SORRY!
AND WHAT'S THE NAME OF OUR CHARMING, NEW NEIGHBOR?
UH... MY NAME'S NINA, SIR!

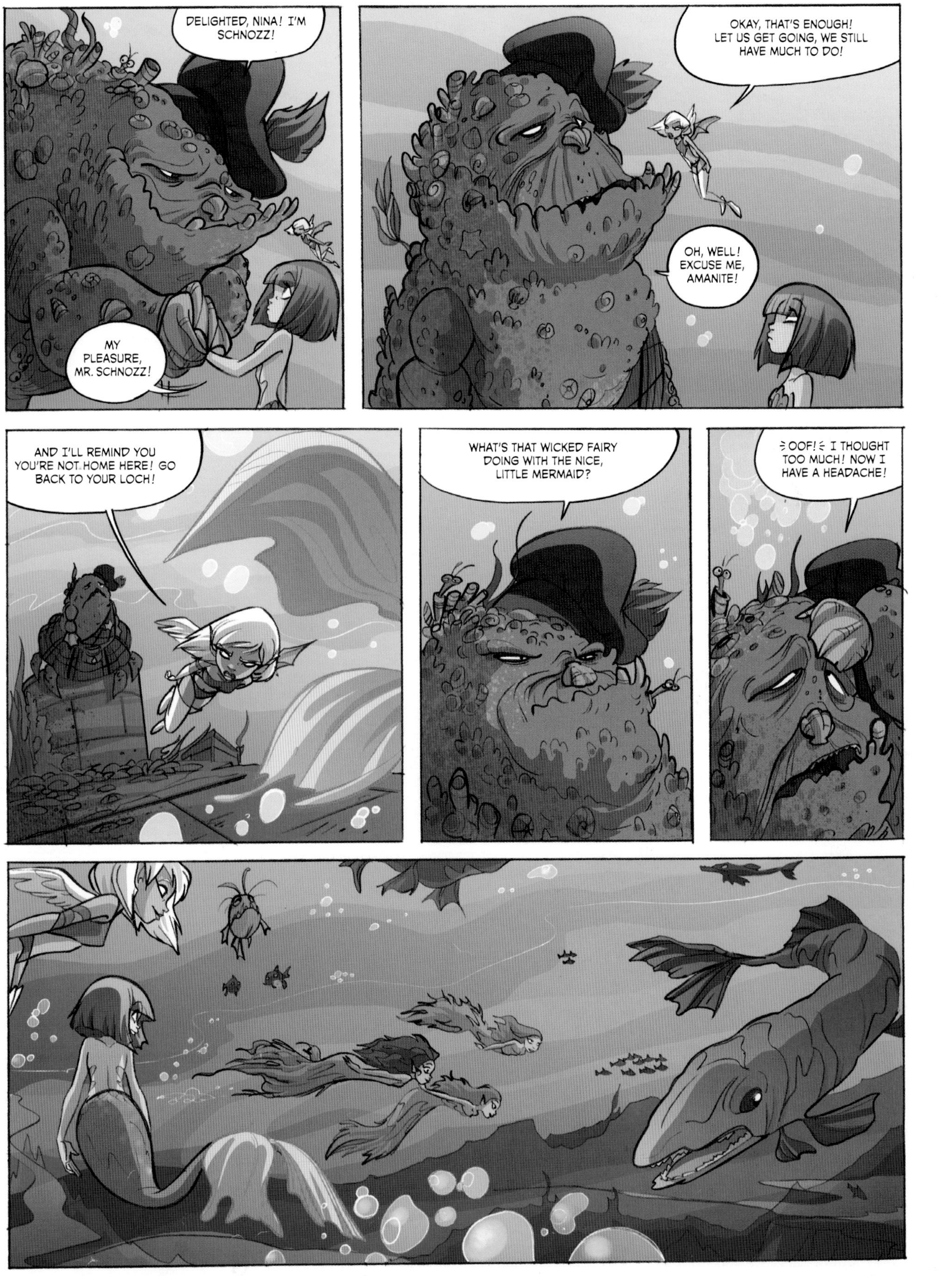
DELIGHTED, NINA! I'M SCHNOZZ!
MY PLEASURE, MR. SCHNOZZ!
OKAY, THAT'S ENOUGH! LET US GET GOING, WE STILL HAVE MUCH TO DO!
OH, WELL! EXCUSE ME, AMANITE!
AND I'LL REMIND YOU YOU'RE NOT HOME HERE! GO BACK TO YOUR LOCH!
WHAT'S THAT WICKED FAIRY DOING WITH THE NICE, LITTLE MERMAID?
OOF! I THOUGHT TOO MUCH! NOW I HAVE A HEADACHE!

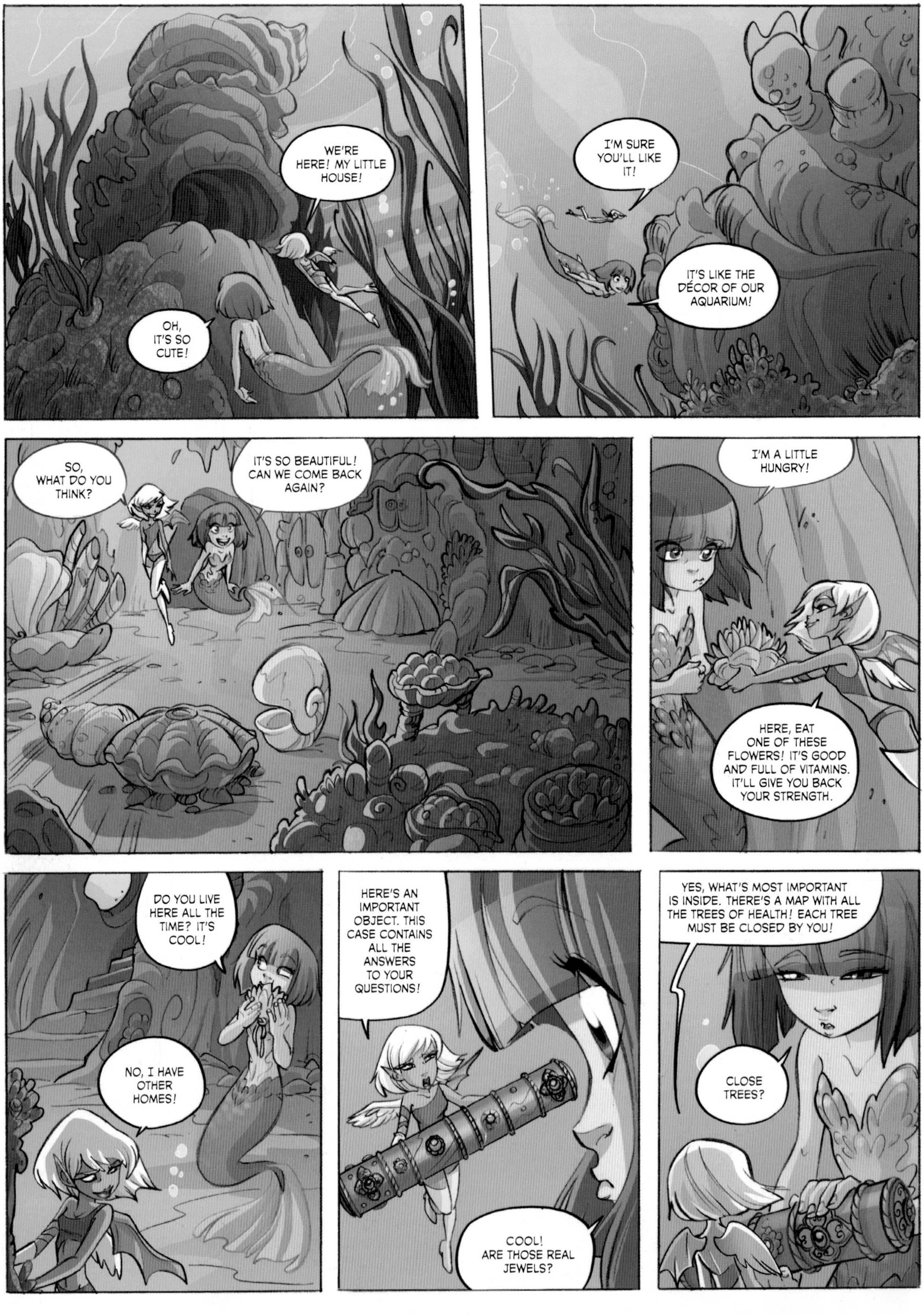
WE'RE HERE! MY LITTLE HOUSE!
OH, IT'S SO CUTE!
I'M SURE YOU'LL LIKE IT!
IT'S LIKE THE DÉCOR OF OUR AQUARIUM!
SO, WHAT DO YOU THINK?
IT'S SO BEAUTIFUL! CAN WE COME BACK AGAIN?
I'M A LITTLE HUNGRY!
HERE, EAT ONE OF THESE FLOWERS! IT'S GOOD AND FULL OF VITAMINS. IT'LL GIVE YOU BACK YOUR STRENGTH.
DO YOU LIVE HERE ALL THE TIME? IT'S COOL!
NO, I HAVE OTHER HOMES!
HERE'S AN IMPORTANT OBJECT. THIS CASE CONTAINS ALL THE ANSWERS TO YOUR QUESTIONS!
COOL! ARE THOSE REAL JEWELS?
YES, WHAT'S MOST IMPORTANT IS INSIDE. THERE'S A MAP WITH ALL THE TREES OF HEALTH! EACH TREE MUST BE CLOSED BY YOU!
CLOSE TREES?

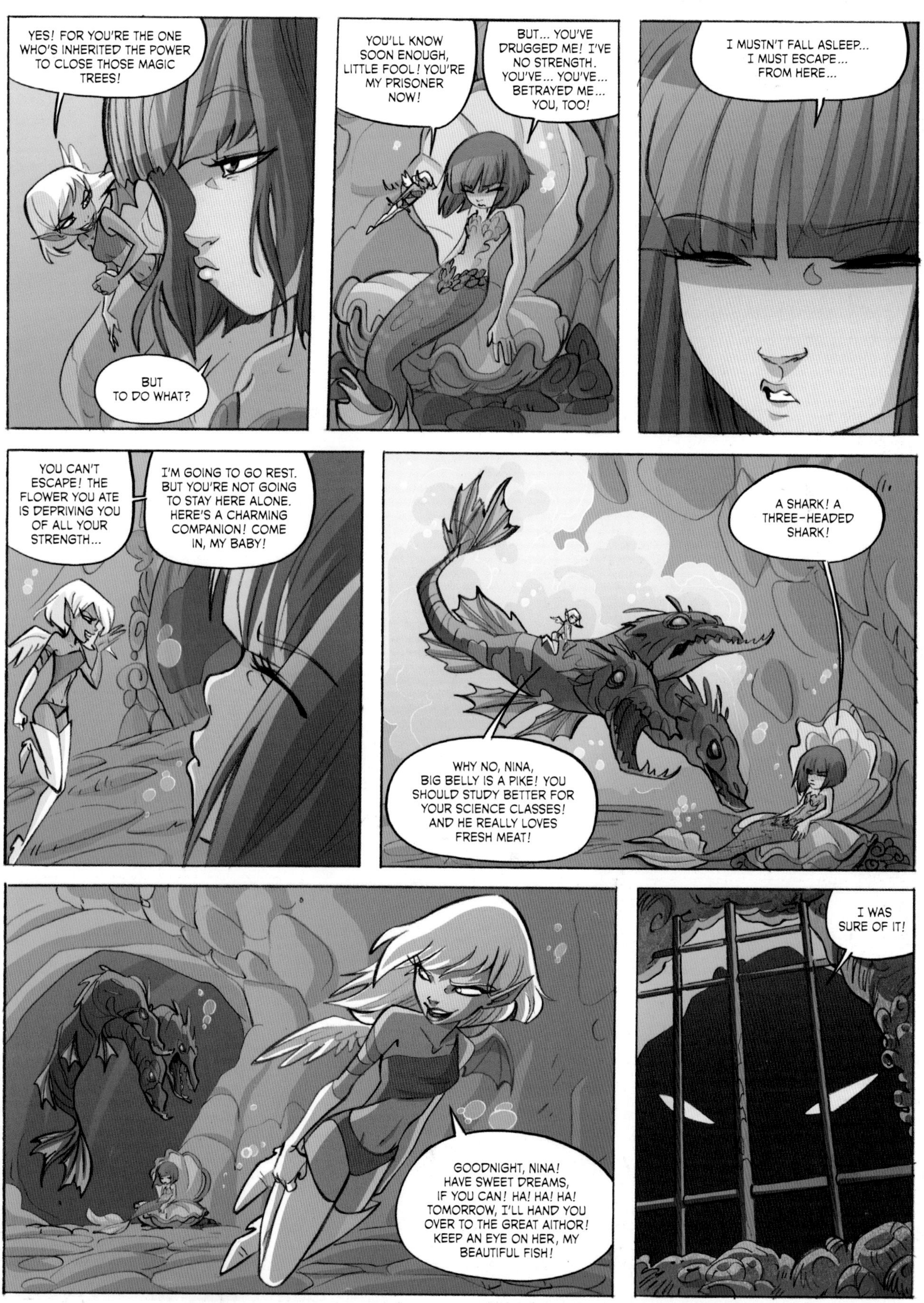
YES! FOR YOU'RE THE ONE WHO'S INHERITED THE POWER TO CLOSE THOSE MAGIC TREES!
BUT TO DO WHAT?
YOU'LL KNOW SOON ENOUGH, LITTLE FOOL! YOU'RE MY PRISONER NOW!
BUT... YOU'VE DRUGGED ME! I'VE NO STRENGTH. YOU'VE... YOU'VE... BETRAYED ME... YOU, TOO!
I MUSTN'T FALL ASLEEP... I MUST ESCAPE... FROM HERE...
YOU CAN'T ESCAPE! THE FLOWER YOU ATE IS DEPRIVING YOU OF ALL YOUR STRENGTH...
I'M GOING TO GO REST. BUT YOU'RE NOT GOING TO STAY HERE ALONE. HERE'S A CHARMING COMPANION! COME IN, MY BABY!
A SHARK! A THREE-HEADED SHARK!
WHY NO, NINA, BIG BELLY IS A PIKE! YOU SHOULD STUDY BETTER FOR YOUR SCIENCE CLASSES! AND HE REALLY LOVES FRESH MEAT!
GOODNIGHT, NINA! HAVE SWEET DREAMS, IF YOU CAN! HA! HA! HA! TOMORROW, I'LL HAND YOU OVER TO THE GREAT AITHOR! KEEP AN EYE ON HER, MY BEAUTIFUL FISH!
I WAS SURE OF IT!

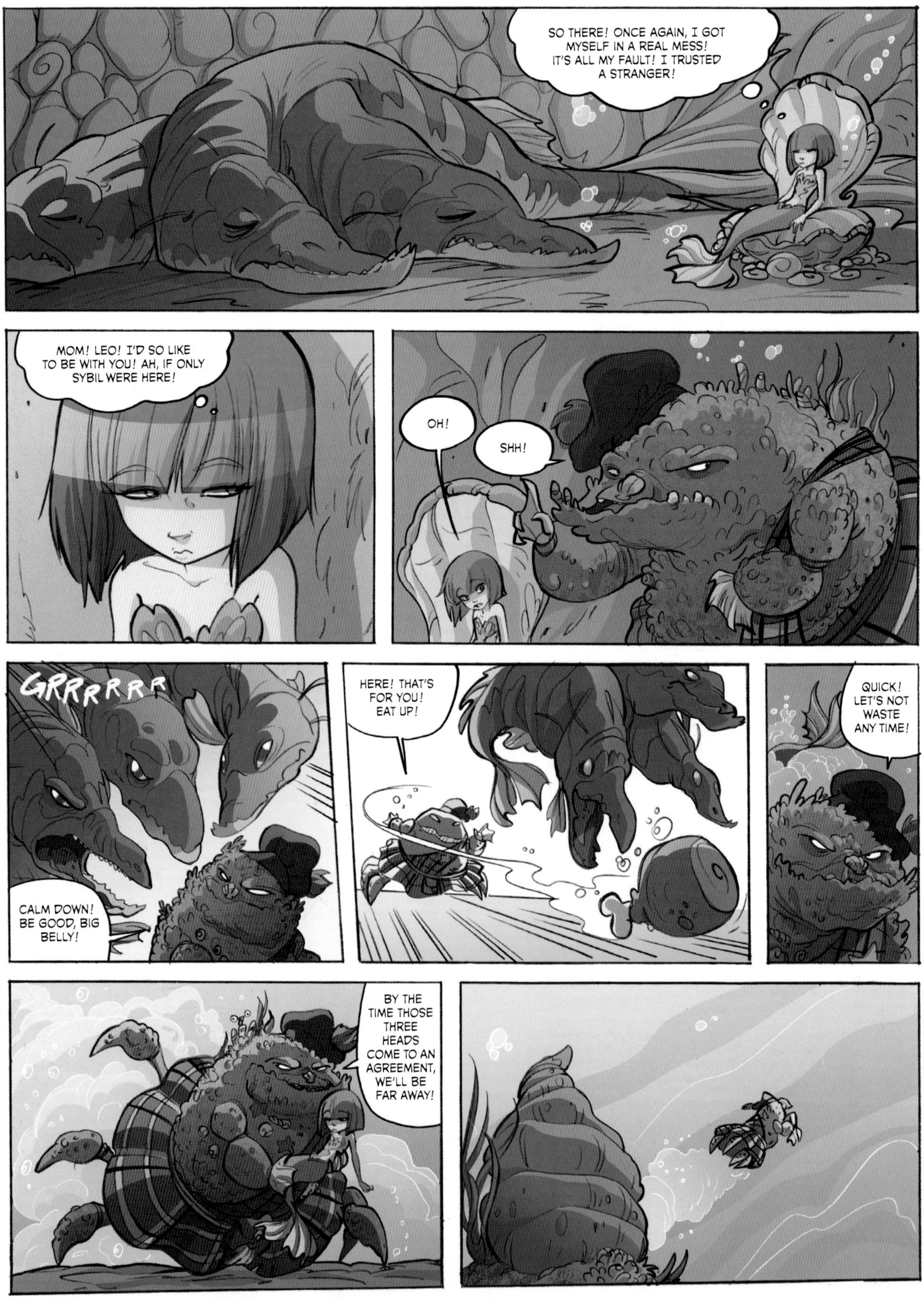
SO THERE! ONCE AGAIN, I GOT MYSELF IN A REAL MESS! IT'S ALL MY FAULT! I TRUSTED A STRANGER!
MOM! LEO! I'D SO LIKE TO BE WITH YOU! AH, IF ONLY SYBIL WERE HERE!
OH!
SHH!
GRRRRRR
CALM DOWN! BE GOOD, BIG BELLY!
HERE! THAT'S FOR YOU! EAT UP!
QUICK! LET'S NOT WASTE ANY TIME!
BY THE TIME THOSE THREE HEADS COME TO AN AGREEMENT, WE'LL BE FAR AWAY!

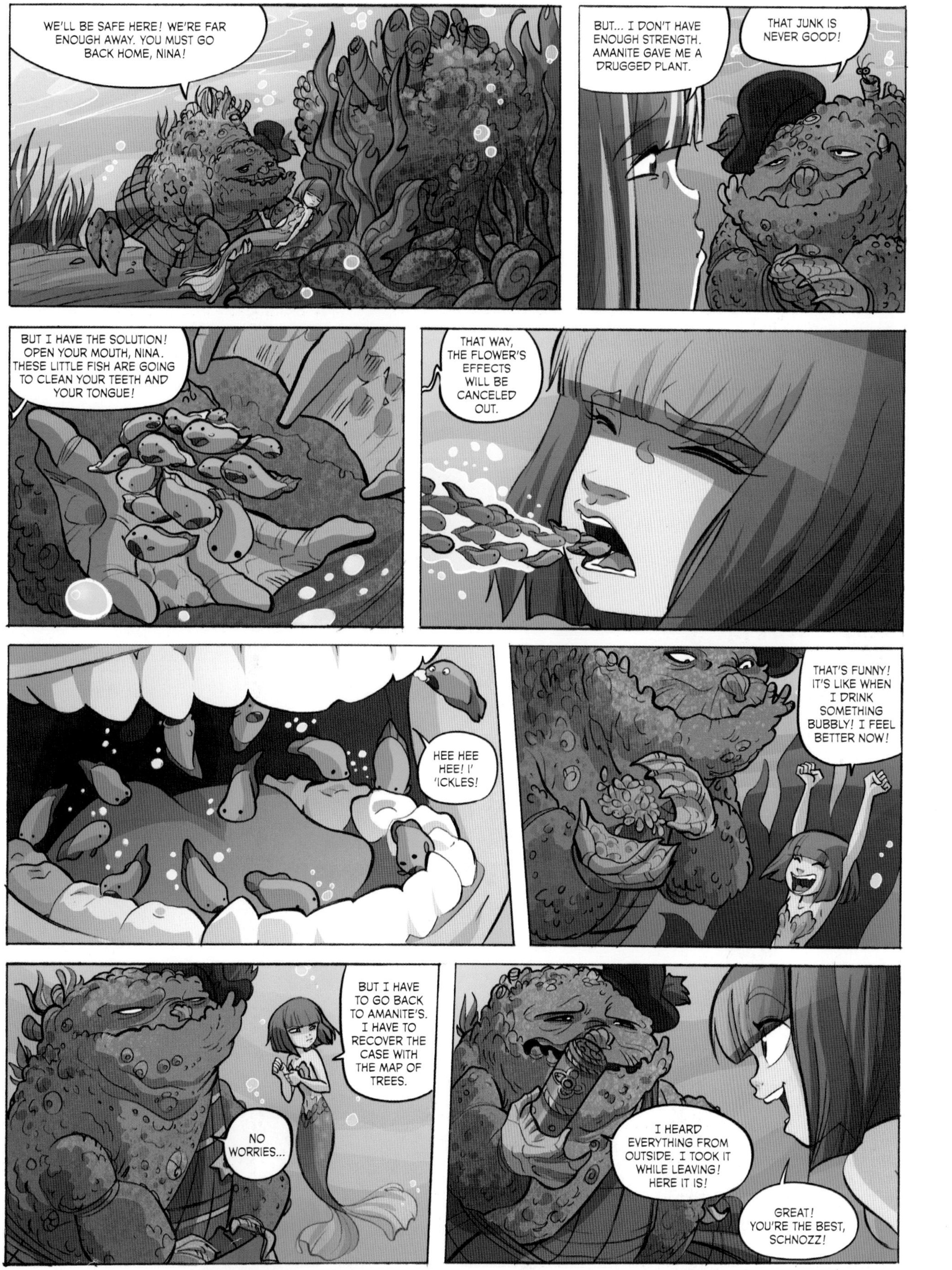
WE'LL BE SAFE HERE! WE'RE FAR ENOUGH AWAY. YOU MUST GO BACK HOME, NINA!
BUT... I DON'T HAVE ENOUGH STRENGTH. AMANITE GAVE ME A DRUGGED PLANT.
THAT JUNK IS NEVER GOOD!
BUT I HAVE THE SOLUTION! OPEN YOUR MOUTH, NINA. THESE LITTLE FISH ARE GOING TO CLEAN YOUR TEETH AND YOUR TONGUE!
THAT WAY, THE FLOWER'S EFFECTS WILL BE CANCELED OUT.
HEE HEE HEE! I' 'ICKLES!
THAT'S FUNNY! IT'S LIKE WHEN I DRINK SOMETHING BUBBLY! I FEEL BETTER NOW!
BUT I HAVE TO GO BACK TO AMANITE'S. I HAVE TO RECOVER THE CASE WITH THE MAP OF TREES.
NO WORRIES...
I HEARD EVERYTHING FROM OUTSIDE. I TOOK IT WHILE LEAVING! HERE IT IS!
GREAT! YOU'RE THE BEST, SCHNOZZ!

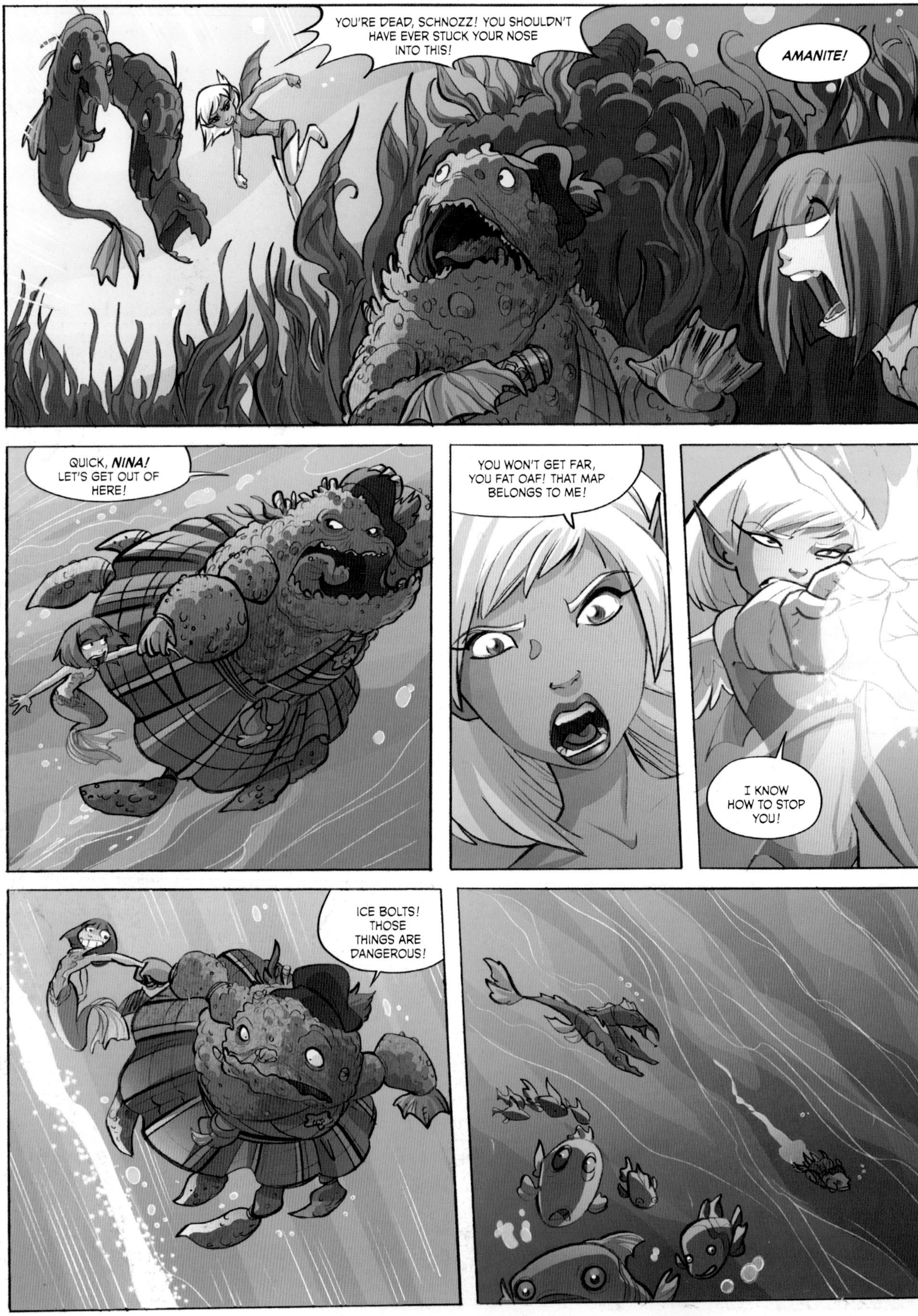
YOU'RE DEAD, SCHNOZZ! YOU SHOULDN'T HAVE EVER STUCK YOUR NOSE INTO THIS!
AMANITE!
QUICK, NINA! LET'S GET OUT OF HERE!
YOU WON'T GET FAR, YOU FAT OAF! THAT MAP BELONGS TO ME!
I KNOW HOW TO STOP YOU!
ICE BOLTS! THOSE THINGS ARE DANGEROUS!

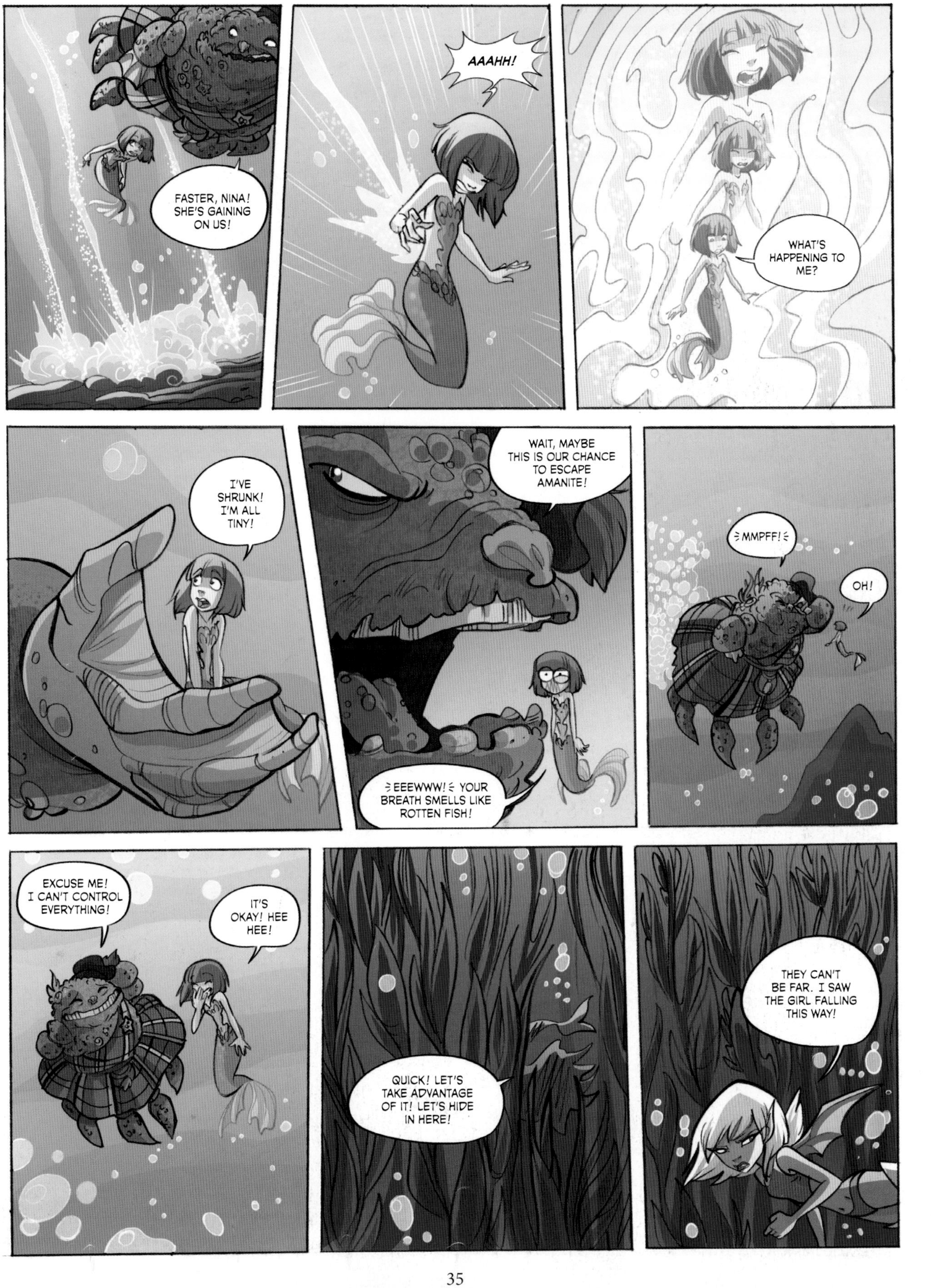
FASTER, NINA! SHE'S GAINING ON US!
AAAHH!
WHAT'S HAPPENING TO ME?
I'VE SHRUNK! I'M ALL TINY!
WAIT, MAYBE THIS IS OUR CHANCE TO ESCAPE AMANITE!
EEEWWW! YOUR BREATH SMELLS LIKE ROTTEN FISH!
MMPFF!
OH!
EXCUSE ME! I CAN'T CONTROL EVERYTHING!
IT'S OKAY! HEE HEE!
QUICK! LET'S TAKE ADVANTAGE OF IT! LET'S HIDE IN HERE!
THEY CAN'T BE FAR. I SAW THE GIRL FALLING THIS WAY!

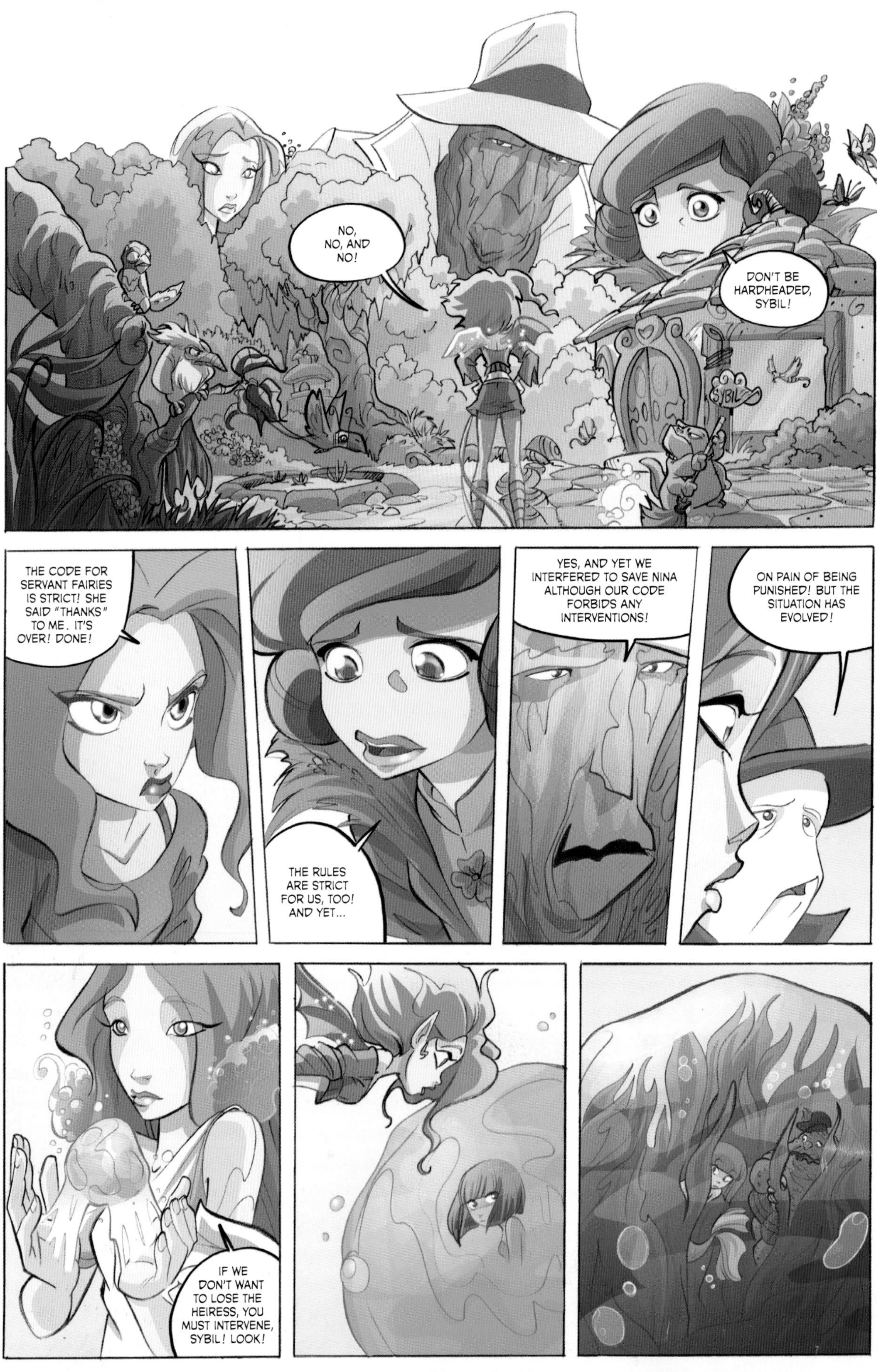
NO, NO, AND NO!
DON'T BE HARDHEADED, SYBIL!
THE CODE FOR SERVANT FAIRIES IS STRICT! SHE SAID "THANKS" TO ME. IT'S OVER! DONE!
THE RULES ARE STRICT FOR US, TOO! AND YET...
YES, AND YET WE INTERFERED TO SAVE NINA ALTHOUGH OUR CODE FORBIDS ANY INTERVENTIONS!
ON PAIN OF BEING PUNISHED! BUT THE SITUATION HAS EVOLVED!
IF WE DON'T WANT TO LOSE THE HEIRESS, YOU MUST INTERVENE, SYBIL! LOOK!

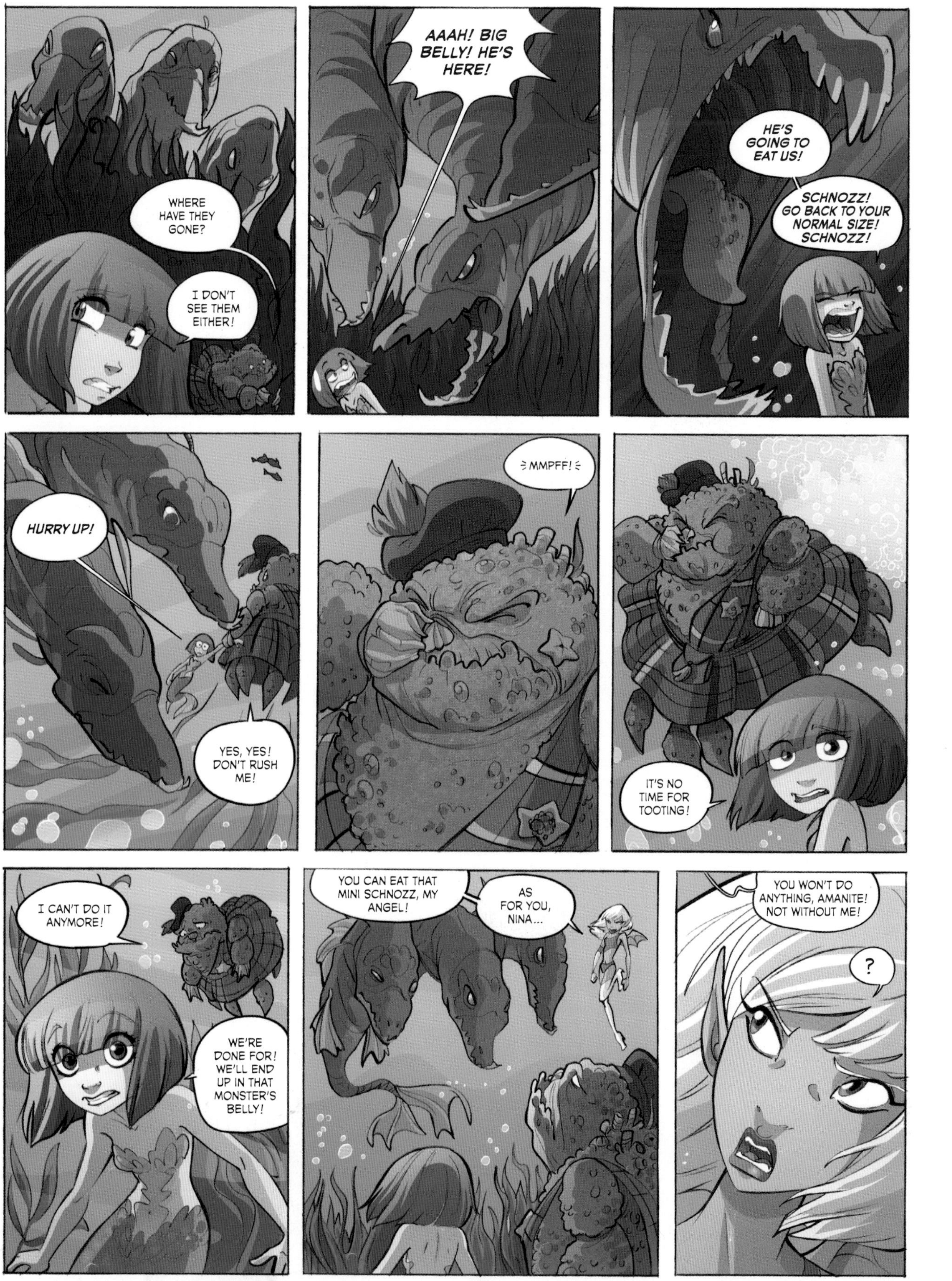
WHERE HAVE THEY GONE?
I DON'T SEE THEM EITHER!
AAAH! BIG BELLY! HE'S HERE!
HE'S GOING TO EAT US!
SCHNOZZ! GO BACK TO YOUR NORMAL SIZE! SCHNOZZ!
HURRY UP!
YES, YES! DON'T RUSH ME!
MMPFF!
IT'S NO TIME FOR TOOTING!
I CAN'T DO IT ANYMORE!
WE'RE DONE FOR! WE'LL END UP IN THAT MONSTER'S BELLY!
YOU CAN EAT THAT MINI SCHNOZZ, MY ANGEL!
AS FOR YOU, NINA...
YOU WON'T DO ANYTHING, AMANITE! NOT WITHOUT ME!
?

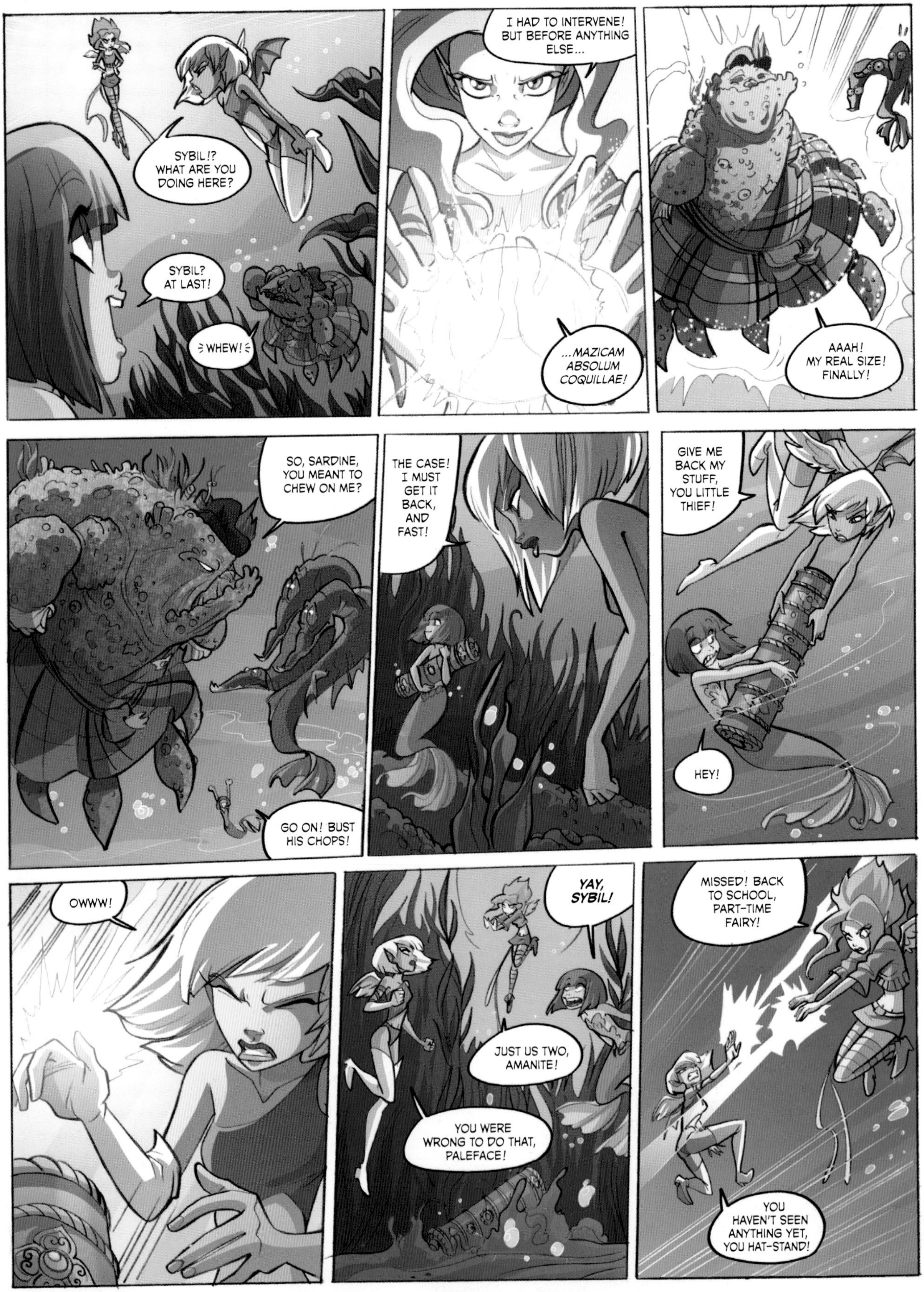
SYBIL!? WHAT ARE YOU DOING HERE?
SYBIL? AT LAST!
WHEW!
I HAD TO INTERVENE! BUT BEFORE ANYTHING ELSE...
...MAZICAM ABSOLUM COQUILLAE!
AAAH! MY REAL SIZE! FINALLY!
SO, SARDINE, YOU MEANT TO CHEW ON ME?
GO ON! BUST HIS CHOPS!
THE CASE! I MUST GET IT BACK, AND FAST!
GIVE ME BACK MY STUFF, YOU LITTLE THIEF!
HEY!
OWWW!
YAY, SYBIL!
JUST US TWO, AMANITE!
YOU WERE WRONG TO DO THAT, PALEFACE!
MISSED! BACK TO SCHOOL, PART-TIME FAIRY!
YOU HAVEN'T SEEN ANYTHING YET, YOU HAT-STAND!

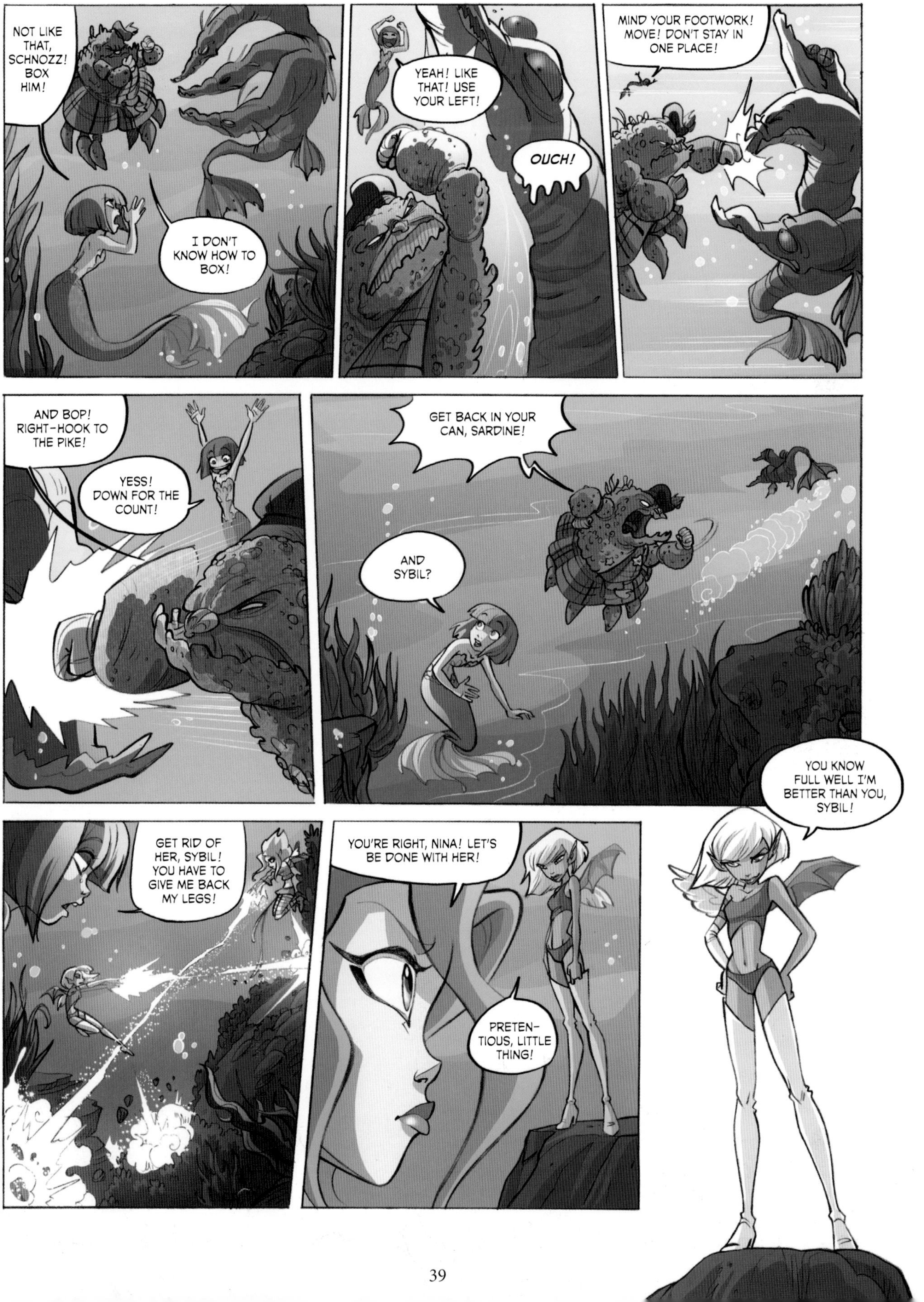
NOT LIKE THAT, SCHNOZZ! BOX HIM!
I DON'T KNOW HOW TO BOX!
YEAH! LIKE THAT! USE YOUR LEFT!
OUCH!
MIND YOUR FOOTWORK! MOVE! DON'T STAY IN ONE PLACE!
AND BOP! RIGHT-HOOK TO THE PIKE!
YESS! DOWN FOR THE COUNT!
GET BACK IN YOUR CAN, SARDINE!
AND SYBIL?
YOU KNOW FULL WELL I'M BETTER THAN YOU, SYBIL!
GET RID OF HER, SYBIL! YOU HAVE TO GIVE ME BACK MY LEGS!
YOU'RE RIGHT, NINA! LET'S BE DONE WITH HER!
PRETEN-TIOUS, LITTLE THING!

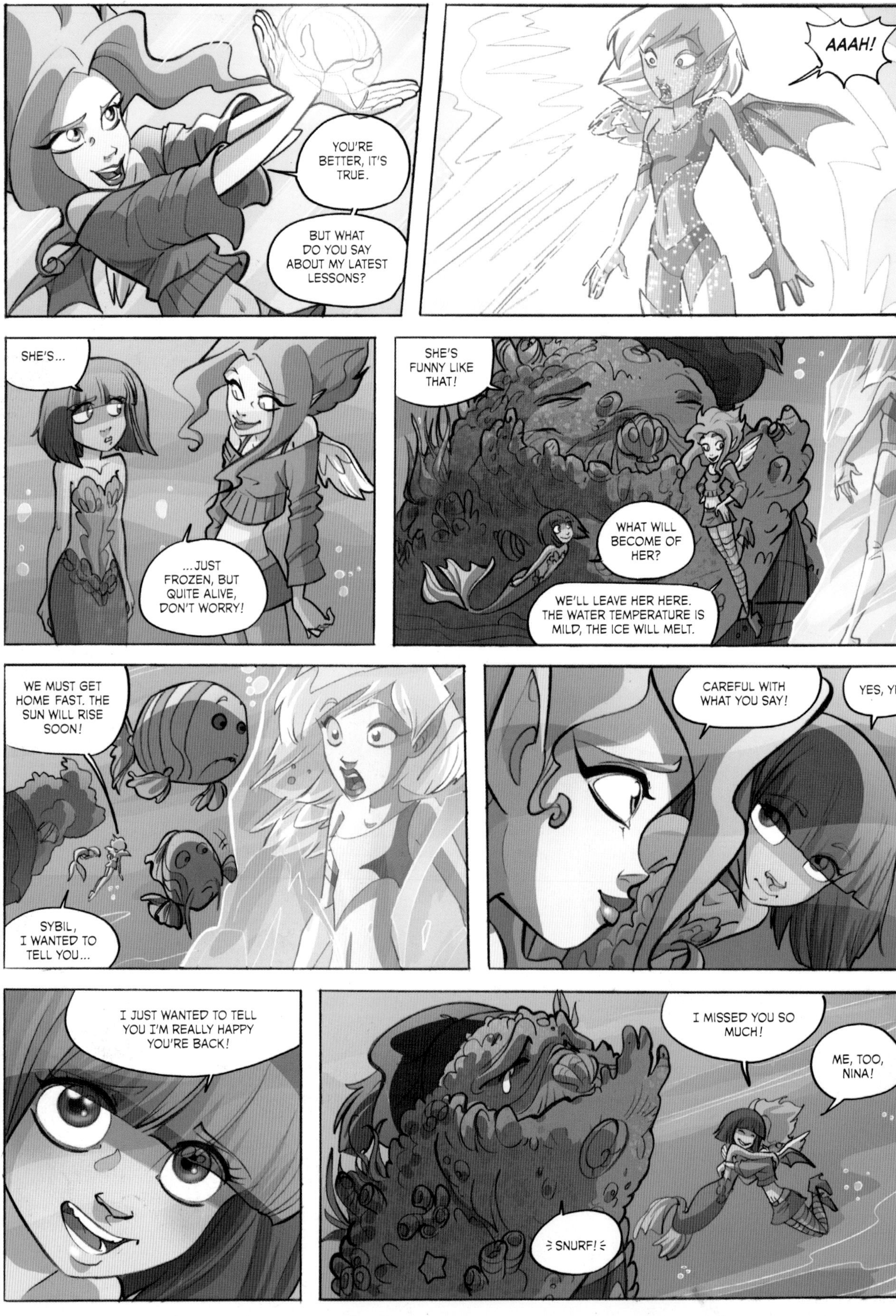
YOU'RE BETTER, IT'S TRUE.
BUT WHAT DO YOU SAY ABOUT MY LATEST LESSONS?
AAAH!
SHE'S...
...JUST FROZEN, BUT QUITE ALIVE, DON'T WORRY!
SHE'S FUNNY LIKE THAT!
WHAT WILL BECOME OF HER?
WE'LL LEAVE HER HERE. THE WATER TEMPERATURE IS MILD, THE ICE WILL MELT.
WE MUST GET HOME FAST. THE SUN WILL RISE SOON!
SYBIL, I WANTED TO TELL YOU...
CAREFUL WITH WHAT YOU SAY!
YES, YES!
I JUST WANTED TO TELL YOU I'M REALLY HAPPY YOU'RE BACK!
I MISSED YOU SO MUCH!
ME, TOO, NINA!
SNURF!

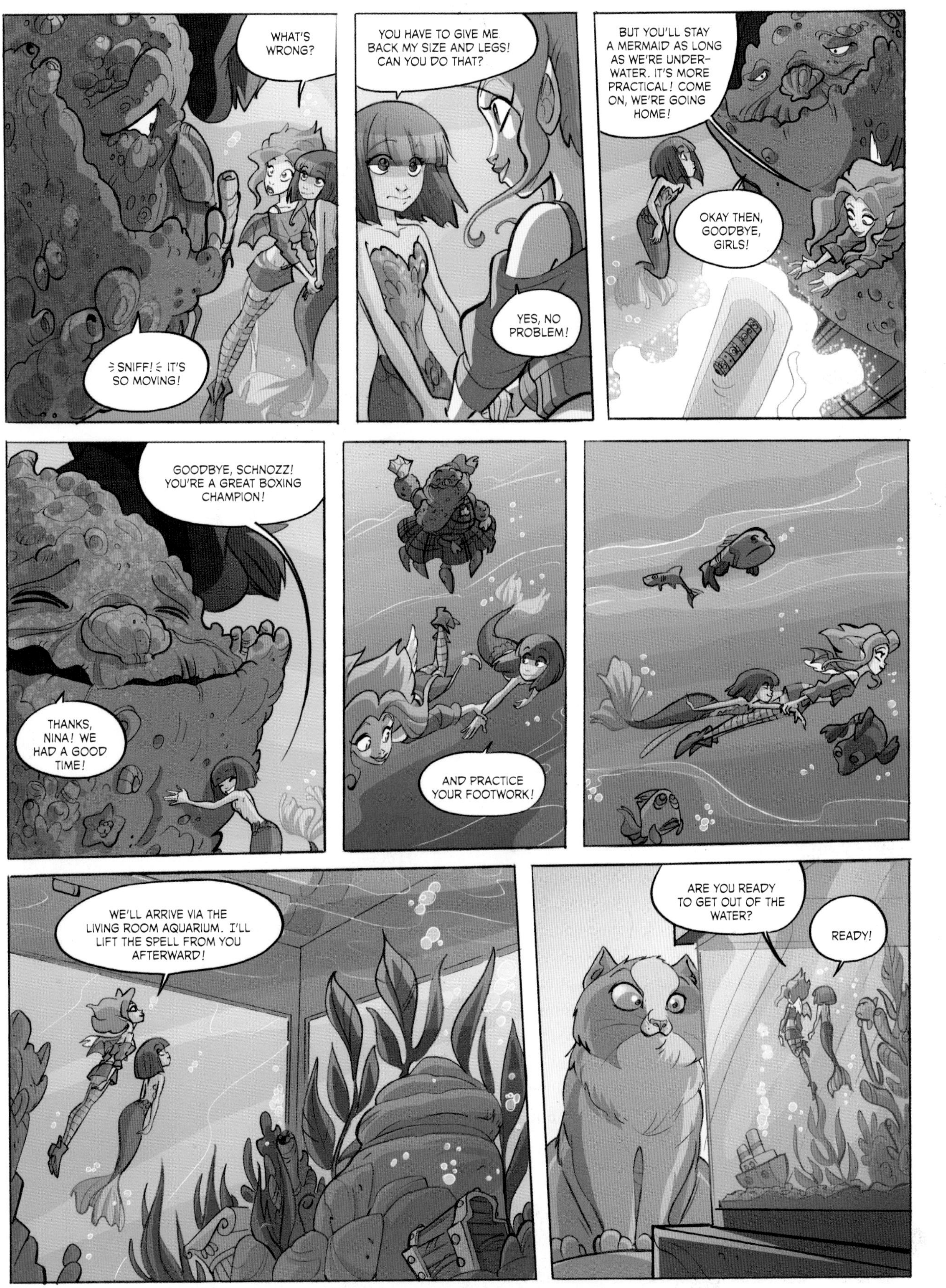
WHAT'S WRONG?
⋚SNIFF!⋛ IT'S SO MOVING!
YOU HAVE TO GIVE ME BACK MY SIZE AND LEGS! CAN YOU DO THAT?
YES, NO PROBLEM!
BUT YOU'LL STAY A MERMAID AS LONG AS WE'RE UNDER-WATER. IT'S MORE PRACTICAL! COME ON, WE'RE GOING HOME!
OKAY THEN, GOODBYE, GIRLS!
GOODBYE, SCHNOZZ! YOU'RE A GREAT BOXING CHAMPION!
THANKS, NINA! WE HAD A GOOD TIME!
AND PRACTICE YOUR FOOTWORK!
WE'LL ARRIVE VIA THE LIVING ROOM AQUARIUM. I'LL LIFT THE SPELL FROM YOU AFTERWARD!
ARE YOU READY TO GET OUT OF THE WATER?
READY!

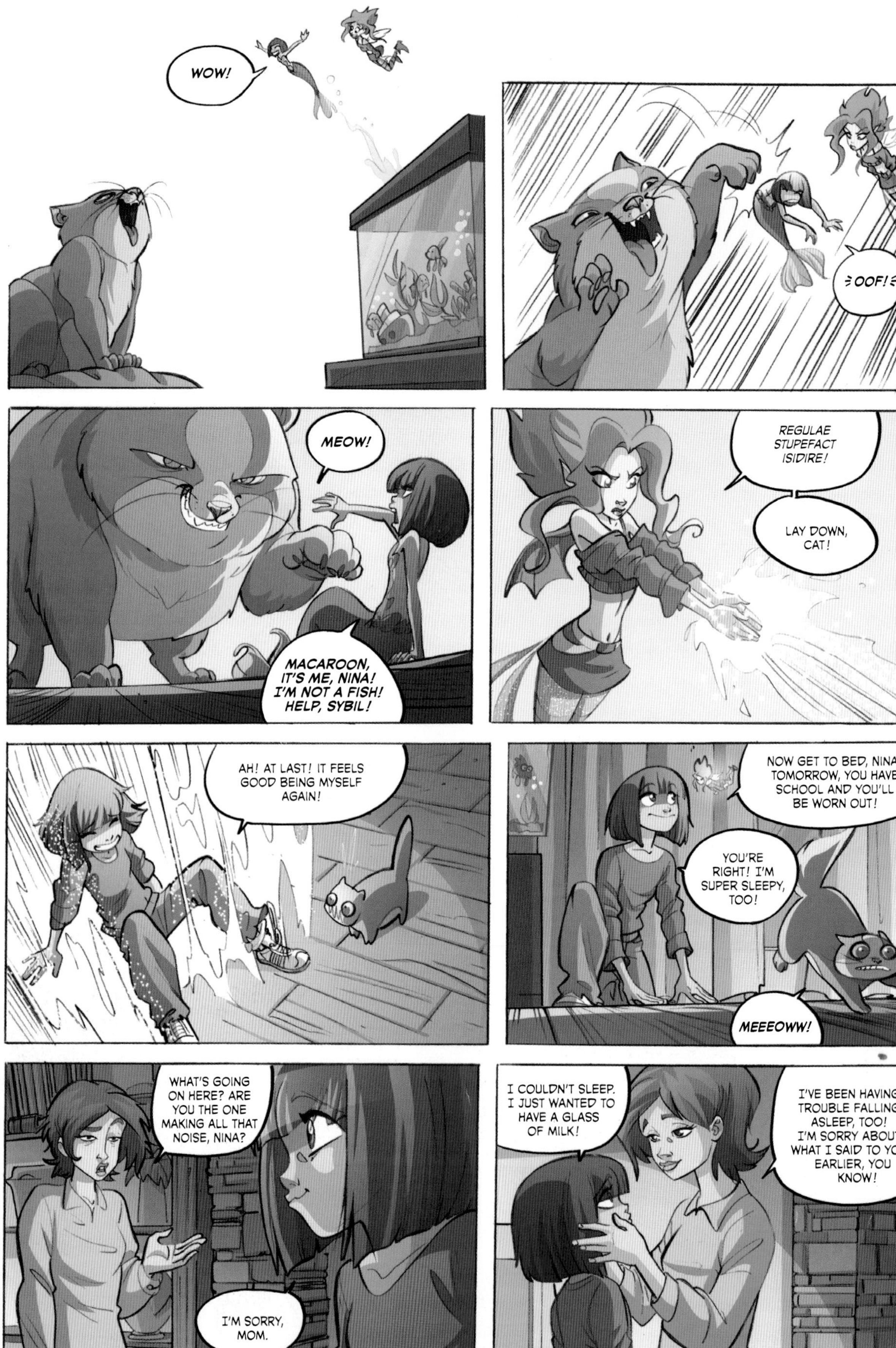
WOW!
OOF!
MEOW!
MACAROON, IT'S ME, NINA! I'M NOT A FISH! HELP, SYBIL!
REGULAE STUPEFACT ISIDIRE!
LAY DOWN, CAT!
AH! AT LAST! IT FEELS GOOD BEING MYSELF AGAIN!
NOW GET TO BED, NINA! TOMORROW, YOU HAVE SCHOOL AND YOU'LL BE WORN OUT!
YOU'RE RIGHT! I'M SUPER SLEEPY, TOO!
MEEEOWW!
WHAT'S GOING ON HERE? ARE YOU THE ONE MAKING ALL THAT NOISE, NINA?
I'M SORRY, MOM.
I COULDN'T SLEEP. I JUST WANTED TO HAVE A GLASS OF MILK!
I'VE BEEN HAVING TROUBLE FALLING ASLEEP, TOO! I'M SORRY ABOUT WHAT I SAID TO YOU EARLIER, YOU KNOW!

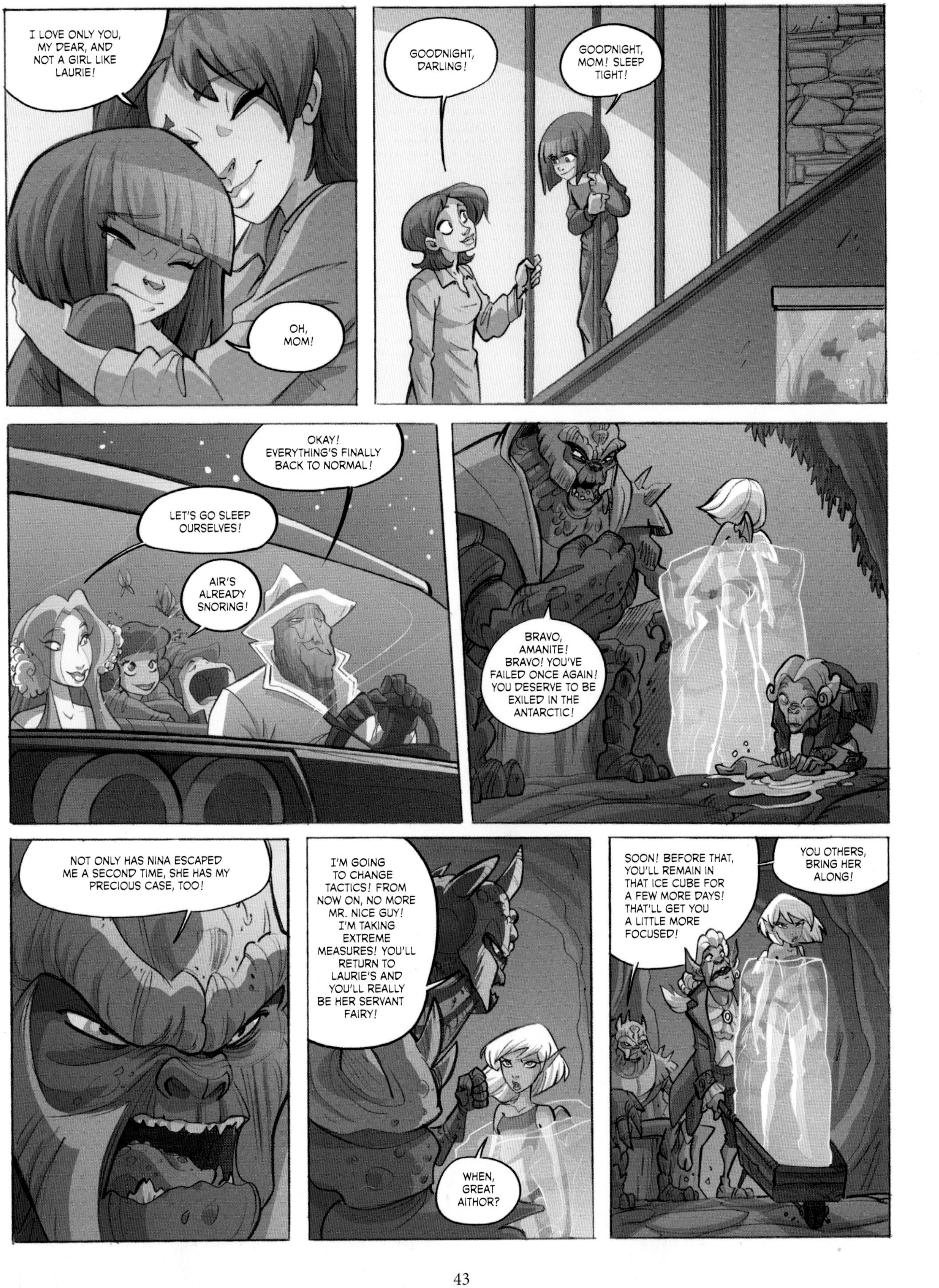
I LOVE ONLY YOU, MY DEAR, AND NOT A GIRL LIKE LAURIE!
OH, MOM!
GOODNIGHT, DARLING!
GOODNIGHT, MOM! SLEEP TIGHT!
OKAY! EVERYTHING'S FINALLY BACK TO NORMAL!
LET'S GO SLEEP OURSELVES!
AIR'S ALREADY SNORING!
BRAVO, AMANITE! BRAVO! YOU'VE FAILED ONCE AGAIN! YOU DESERVE TO BE EXILED IN THE ANTARCTIC!
NOT ONLY HAS NINA ESCAPED ME A SECOND TIME, SHE HAS MY PRECIOUS CASE, TOO!
I'M GOING TO CHANGE TACTICS! FROM NOW ON, NO MORE MR. NICE GUY! I'M TAKING EXTREME MEASURES! YOU'LL RETURN TO LAURIE'S AND YOU'LL REALLY BE HER SERVANT FAIRY!
WHEN, GREAT AITHOR?
SOON! BEFORE THAT, YOU'LL REMAIN IN THAT ICE CUBE FOR A FEW MORE DAYS! THAT'LL GET YOU A LITTLE MORE FOCUSED!
YOU OTHERS, BRING HER ALONG!

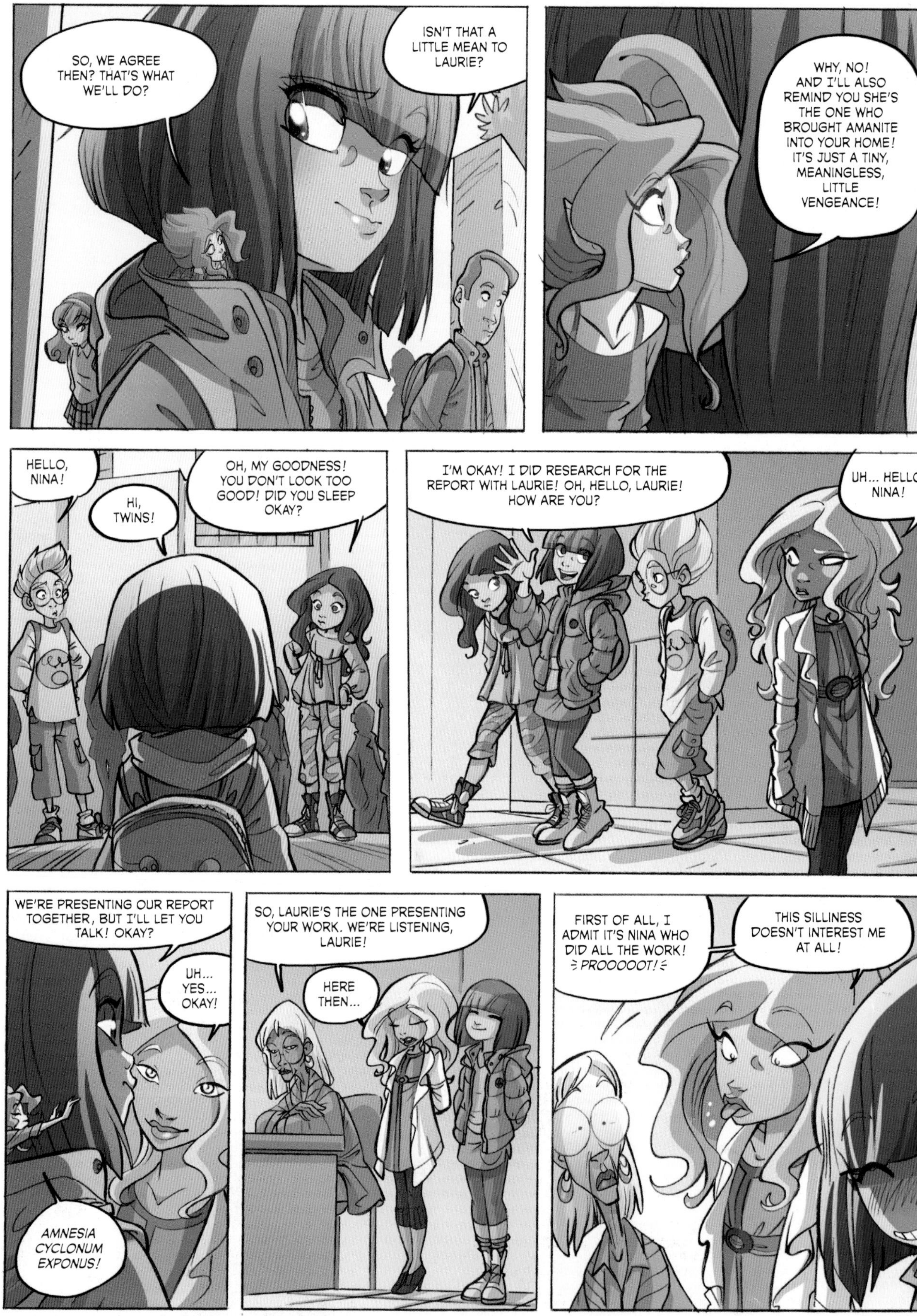

SO, WE AGREE THEN? THAT'S WHAT WE'LL DO?
ISN'T THAT A LITTLE MEAN TO LAURIE?
WHY, NO! AND I'LL ALSO REMIND YOU SHE'S THE ONE WHO BROUGHT AMANITE INTO YOUR HOME! IT'S JUST A TINY, MEANINGLESS, LITTLE VENGEANCE!
HELLO, NINA!
HI, TWINS!
OH, MY GOODNESS! YOU DON'T LOOK TOO GOOD! DID YOU SLEEP OKAY?
I'M OKAY! I DID RESEARCH FOR THE REPORT WITH LAURIE! OH, HELLO, LAURIE! HOW ARE YOU?
UH... HELLO, NINA!
WE'RE PRESENTING OUR REPORT TOGETHER, BUT I'LL LET YOU TALK! OKAY?
UH... YES... OKAY!
AMNESIA CYCLONUM EXPONUS!
SO, LAURIE'S THE ONE PRESENTING YOUR WORK. WE'RE LISTENING, LAURIE!
HERE THEN...
FIRST OF ALL, I ADMIT IT'S NINA WHO DID ALL THE WORK! PROOOOOT!
THIS SILLINESS DOESN'T INTEREST ME AT ALL!

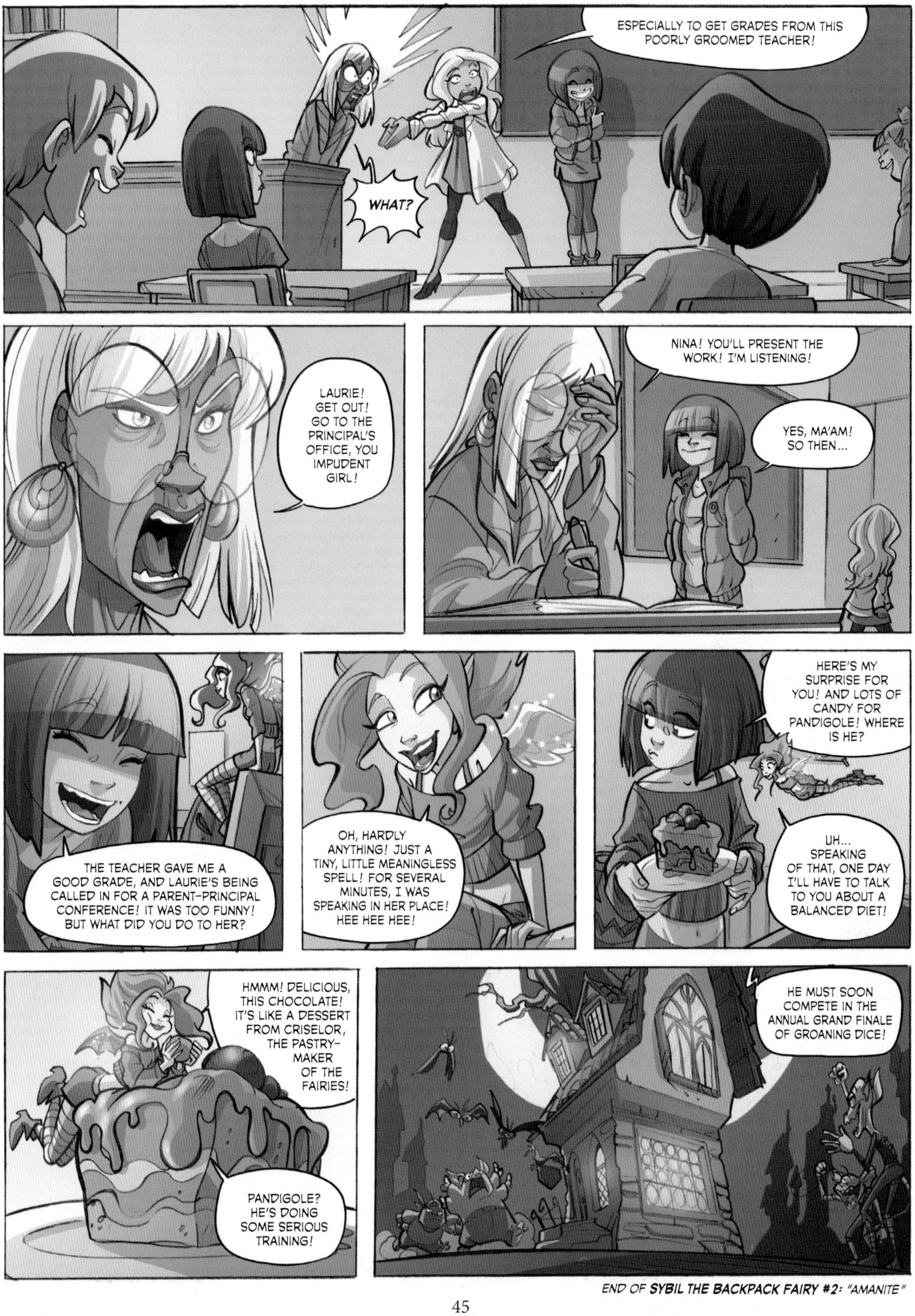

ESPECIALLY TO GET GRADES FROM THIS POORLY GROOMED TEACHER!
WHAT?
LAURIE! GET OUT! GO TO THE PRINCIPAL'S OFFICE, YOU IMPUDENT GIRL!
NINA! YOU'LL PRESENT THE WORK! I'M LISTENING!
YES, MA'AM! SO THEN...
THE TEACHER GAVE ME A GOOD GRADE, AND LAURIE'S BEING CALLED IN FOR A PARENT-PRINCIPAL CONFERENCE! IT WAS TOO FUNNY! BUT WHAT DID YOU DO TO HER?
OH, HARDLY ANYTHING! JUST A TINY, LITTLE MEANINGLESS SPELL! FOR SEVERAL MINUTES, I WAS SPEAKING IN HER PLACE! HEE HEE HEE!
HERE'S MY SURPRISE FOR YOU! AND LOTS OF CANDY FOR PANDIGOLE! WHERE IS HE?
UH... SPEAKING OF THAT, ONE DAY I'LL HAVE TO TALK TO YOU ABOUT A BALANCED DIET!
HMMM! DELICIOUS, THIS CHOCOLATE! IT'S LIKE A DESSERT FROM CRISELOR, THE PASTRY-MAKER OF THE FAIRIES!
PANDIGOLE? HE'S DOING SOME SERIOUS TRAINING!
HE MUST SOON COMPETE IN THE ANNUAL GRAND FINALE OF GROANING DICE!

END OF **SYBIL THE BACKPACK FAIRY #2**: "AMANITE"

As a bonus, here are a few scenes from my new life with

SYBIL the Backpack Fairy

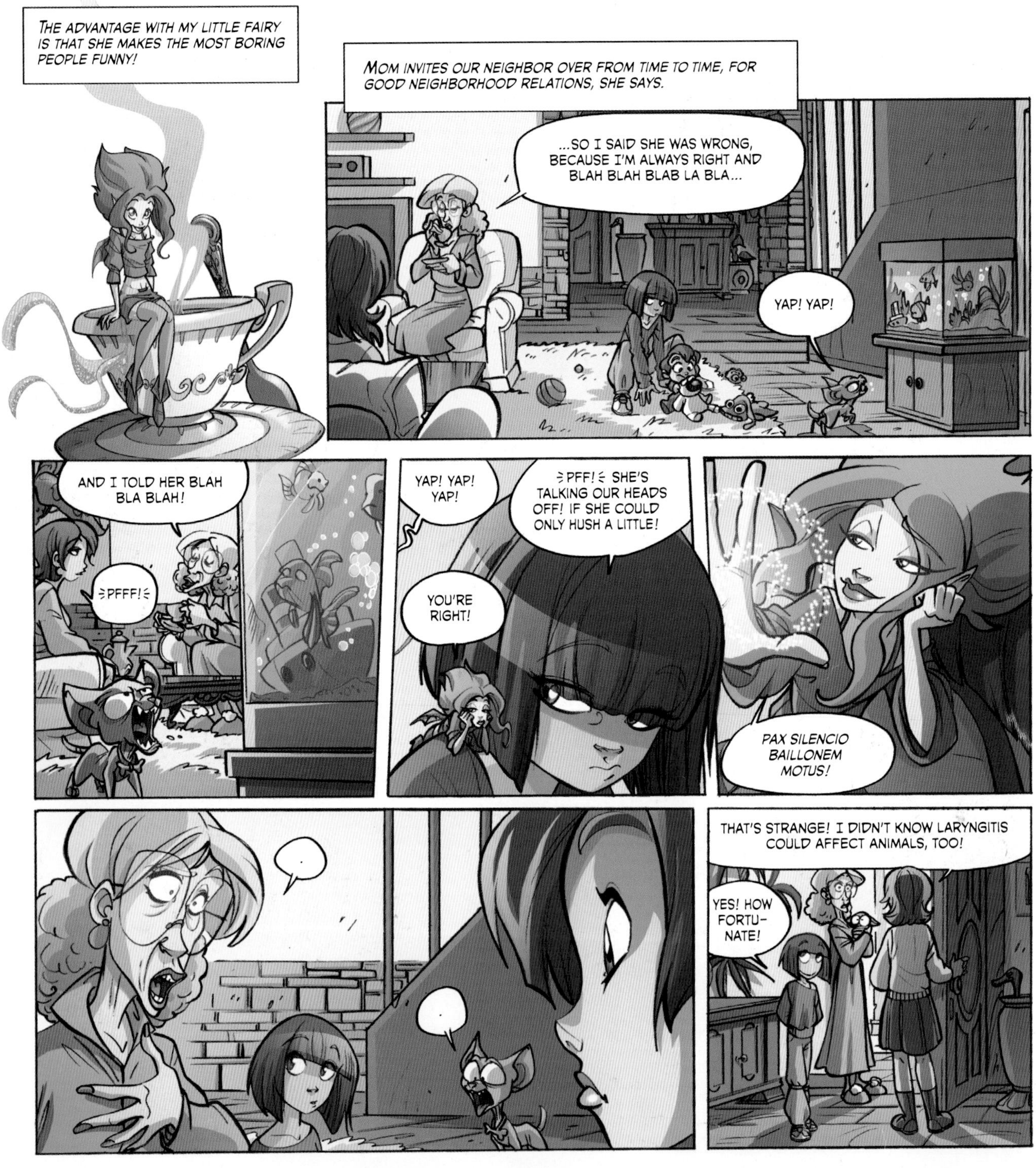

THE ADVANTAGE WITH MY LITTLE FAIRY IS THAT SHE MAKES THE MOST BORING PEOPLE FUNNY!
MOM INVITES OUR NEIGHBOR OVER FROM TIME TO TIME, FOR GOOD NEIGHBORHOOD RELATIONS, SHE SAYS.
...SO I SAID SHE WAS WRONG, BECAUSE I'M ALWAYS RIGHT AND BLAH BLAH BLAB LA BLA...
YAP! YAP!
AND I TOLD HER BLAH BLA BLAH!
PFFF!
YAP! YAP! YAP!
PFF! SHE'S TALKING OUR HEADS OFF! IF SHE COULD ONLY HUSH A LITTLE!
YOU'RE RIGHT!
PAX SILENCIO BAILLONEM MOTUS!
THAT'S STRANGE! I DIDN'T KNOW LARYNGITIS COULD AFFECT ANIMALS, TOO!
YES! HOW FORTU-NATE!

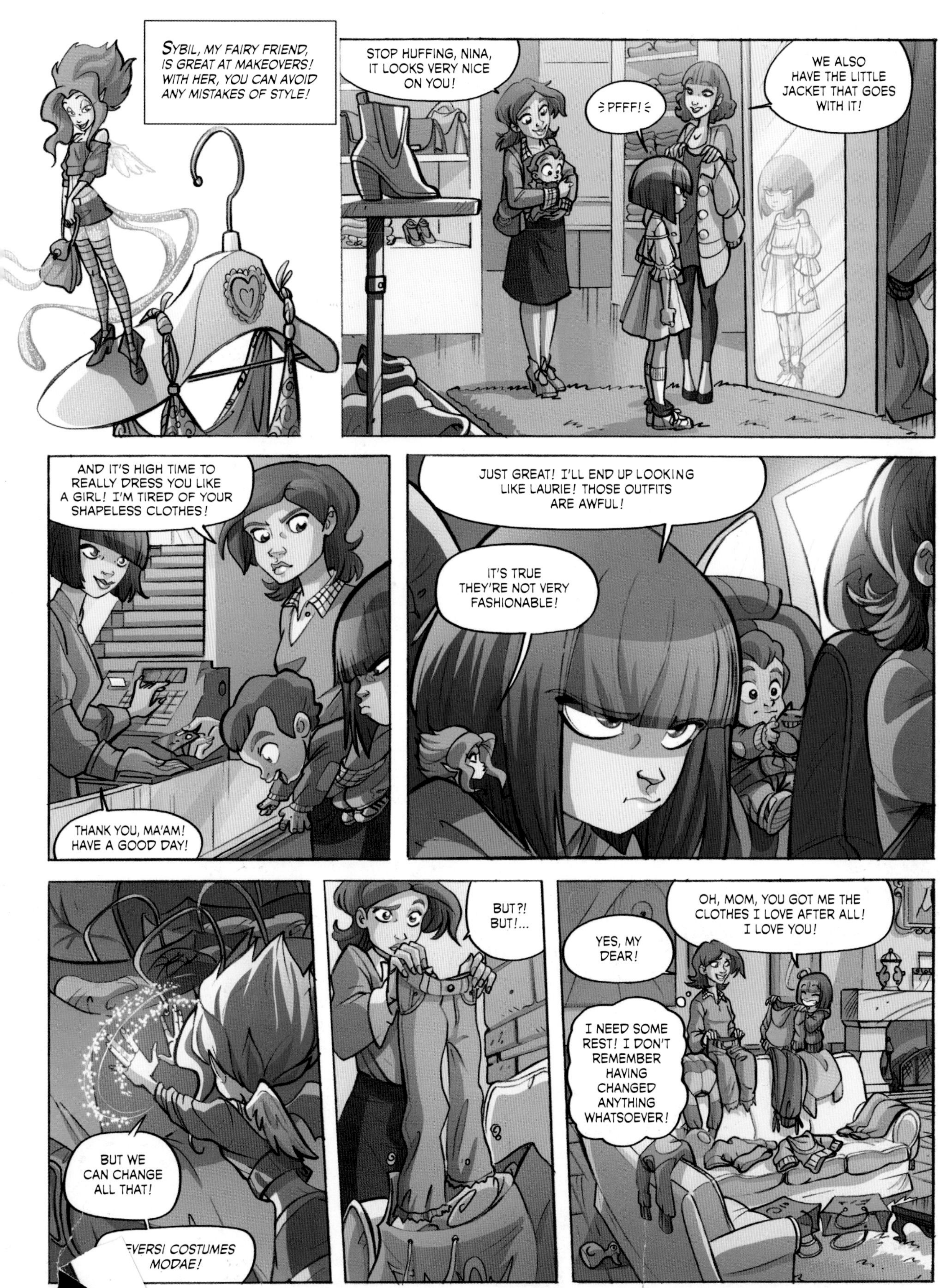
SYBIL, MY FAIRY FRIEND, IS GREAT AT MAKEOVERS! WITH HER, YOU CAN AVOID ANY MISTAKES OF STYLE!
STOP HUFFING, NINA, IT LOOKS VERY NICE ON YOU!
PFFF!
WE ALSO HAVE THE LITTLE JACKET THAT GOES WITH IT!
AND IT'S HIGH TIME TO REALLY DRESS YOU LIKE A GIRL! I'M TIRED OF YOUR SHAPELESS CLOTHES!
THANK YOU, MA'AM! HAVE A GOOD DAY!
JUST GREAT! I'LL END UP LOOKING LIKE LAURIE! THOSE OUTFITS ARE AWFUL!
IT'S TRUE THEY'RE NOT VERY FASHIONABLE!
BUT WE CAN CHANGE ALL THAT!
EVERSI COSTUMES MODAE!
BUT?! BUT!...
OH, MOM, YOU GOT ME THE CLOTHES I LOVE AFTER ALL! I LOVE YOU!
YES, MY DEAR!
I NEED SOME REST! I DON'T REMEMBER HAVING CHANGED ANYTHING WHATSOEVER!

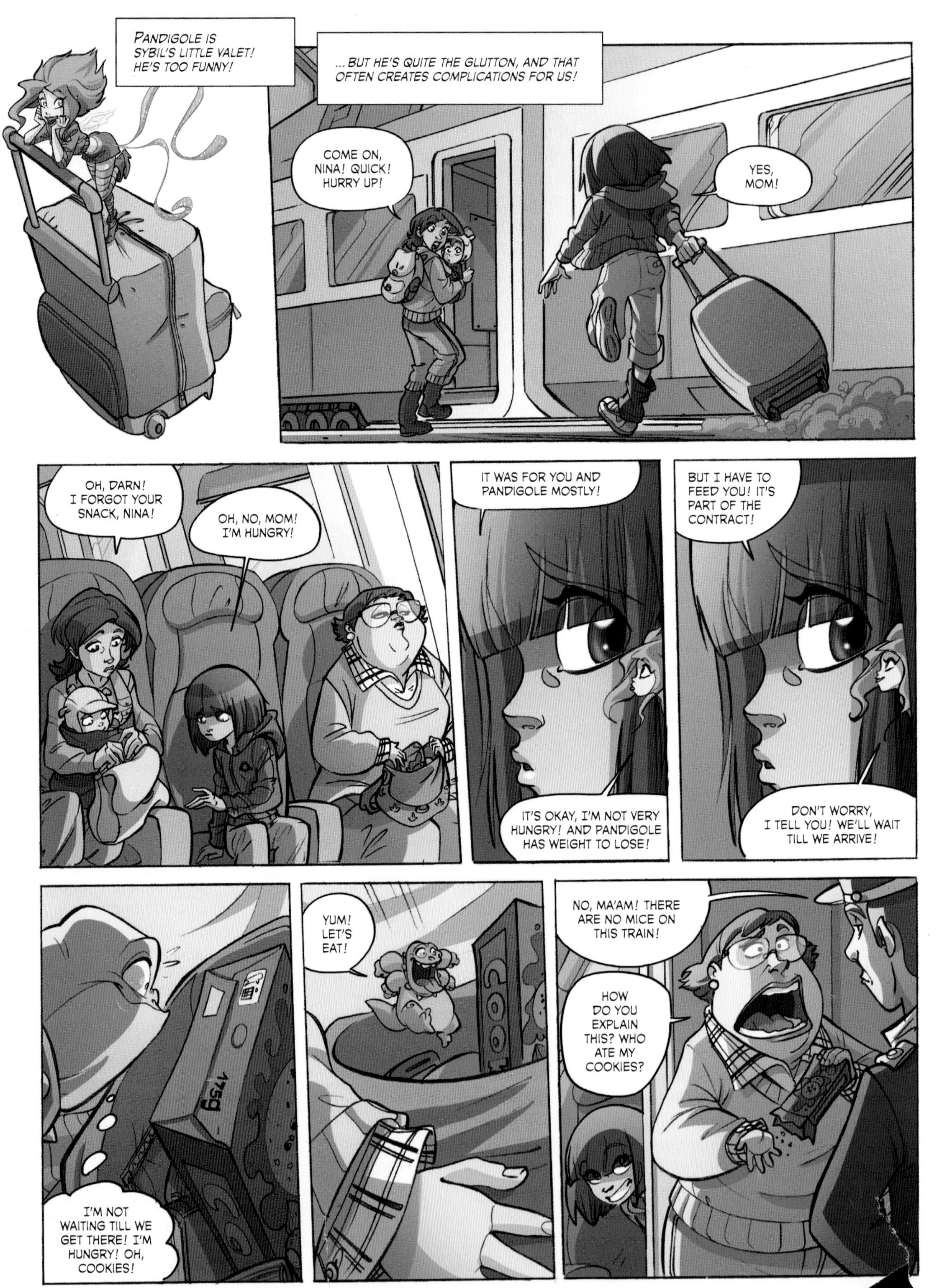
PANDIGOLE IS SYBIL'S LITTLE VALET! HE'S TOO FUNNY!
... BUT HE'S QUITE THE GLUTTON, AND THAT OFTEN CREATES COMPLICATIONS FOR US!
COME ON, NINA! QUICK! HURRY UP!
YES, MOM!
OH, DARN! I FORGOT YOUR SNACK, NINA!
OH, NO, MOM! I'M HUNGRY!
IT WAS FOR YOU AND PANDIGOLE MOSTLY!
IT'S OKAY, I'M NOT VERY HUNGRY! AND PANDIGOLE HAS WEIGHT TO LOSE!
BUT I HAVE TO FEED YOU! IT'S PART OF THE CONTRACT!
DON'T WORRY, I TELL YOU! WE'LL WAIT TILL WE ARRIVE!
175g
I'M NOT WAITING TILL WE GET THERE! I'M HUNGRY! OH, COOKIES!
YUM! LET'S EAT!
NO, MA'AM! THERE ARE NO MICE ON THIS TRAIN!
HOW DO YOU EXPLAIN THIS? WHO ATE MY COOKIES?